Other Books by
LENSEY NAMIOKA

THE SAMURAI AND THE LONG-NOSED DEVILS

WHITE SERPENT CASTLE

VALLEY OF THE BROKEN CHERRY TREES

VILLAGE OF
THE VAMPIRE CAT

Lensey Namioka

DELACORTE PRESS/NEW YORK

Published by
Delacorte Press
1 Dag Hammarskjold Plaza
New York, N.Y. 10017

Manufactured in the United States of America

First printing

LIBRARY OF CONGRESS CATALOGING IN PUBLICATION DATA

Namioka, Lensey.
Village of the vampire cat.

SUMMARY: When a young ronin returns to the
village of his former teacher, he and his companion
find it being terrorized by a mysterious killer.
[1. Samurai—Fiction. 2. Japan—Fiction]
I.   Title.
PZ7.N1426Vi   [Fic]   80-68737
ISBN 0-440-09377-5

To my husband,
who put up patiently with
all that *chambara*.

List of Characters for
VILLAGE OF THE VAMPIRE CAT

Zenta—a young ronin (unemployed samurai)
Matsuzo—Zenta's traveling companion
Ikken—a tea ceremony master
Shunken—Ikken's son, killed in battle
Toshi—widow of Ikken's brother
Asa—Toshi's daughter
Ryutaro—the leader of an outlaw band
Hirobei—a merchant and Toshi's business manager
Jiro—village carpenter
Kiku—Jiro's daughter
Tavern keeper
Tavern keeper's wife
An exorcist
Kongomaru—Asa's dog

1

The two travelers paused at the end of the street and looked around them in dismay. Even the falling snow couldn't hide the wretchedness of the village. On both sides of the street the walls of the houses showed large patches of crumbling plaster, and their plank roofs sagged under thick quilts of snow. A gust of wind flapped the torn paper in the windows.

Zenta, the taller of the two travelers, shivered and pulled his cloak about him. The two swords of the samurai protruded from the folds of his cloak, but no warlord's insignia showed on his clothes, for he was a *ronin*, a masterless samurai. Brushing the snow from his eyes, he said, "I don't remember the village looking like this at all. We must have come to the wrong place!"

Matsuzo, his companion, shifted the heavy pack on his back and stamped his feet. He could feel the cold seeping through his thick straw boots. A few years younger than Zenta, he was not so used to the harsh life of a wandering ronin. After traveling all day he was cold, hungry, and footsore. "It's been almost ten years since you visited this village," he pointed out. "It must have changed a lot. You told me there was a fierce battle here three years ago. The houses were probably damaged during the fighting."

The two travelers walked slowly down the street and inspected the silent houses on either side of them. They could feel wary eyes watching them behind the gaping windows.

"I don't think these conditions were caused by the fighting," Zenta said finally. "The villagers could have repaired the damage. Or if it had been very bad, they would have abandoned the place. No, the people here have been letting things slowly fall apart."

Looking around at the signs of decay, Matsuzo was forced to agree. "Whatever the reason for the misery, we won't find any warmth or shelter here. Let's hurry to Ikken's house. I hope he isn't affected by the general misfortune."

Ikken, a tea master, was the person they had traveled here to see. Ten years ago, when he was fifteen, Zenta had studied the tea ceremony under Ikken. Now he was revisiting his old teacher and bringing with him gifts of wine and food, special delicacies of the New Year season.

In addition he was bringing a far more valuable gift, a clay tea bowl that had belonged to a wealthy warlord. In order to obtain this bowl Zenta had worked for months as instructor in swordsmanship to the warlord's spoiled son.

The tea master's house was in the hills a little distance from the village. But before the two men reached the last of the village houses and started the climb uphill, Zenta suddenly stopped. "Wait! Here is one place that still looks the same."

It was a tavern, and in the decaying village it was the only place with any sign of prosperity. A cheerful yellow light showed through the neatly papered front windows. From the back of the house came the unmistakable thud of wooden mallets pounding on a tub of glutinous rice. Any house that could afford to make New Year's rice cakes would not be too badly off.

"Let's stop here for a drink," said Zenta, sliding open the front door of the tavern.

Surprised, Matsuzo peered into the tavern and saw a small room with a floor of beaten earth and crude wooden benches for the customers. The benches were empty, and though the place was less dilapidated than the rest of the village, Matsuzo saw nothing there to attract him. "I don't see why you want to stop. We're carrying excellent sake in our luggage, better than anything we can get here."

Zenta ignored Matsuzo's words. "I wonder if the owner is still here. Yes, there he is. He hasn't changed much after all these years. Come on."

Following his companion into the tavern, Matsuzo looked curiously at the owner and wondered at Zenta's eagerness to visit him. The tavern owner was a short man with a big head thrust slightly forward. He must be cunning, Matsuzo thought, to remain prosperous while the rest of the village starved. The young ronin read greed in the man's small bright eyes and tightly pursed mouth.

The owner looked up with a frown as the two men walked in. Hurrying forward to welcome his customers, he changed his frown into a smile. He showed no sign of recognizing Zenta. His eyes widened, however, at the sight of his customers' swords, which he considered thoughtfully for a moment before turning away to fetch the wine.

The two ronin removed their packs, took off their hats and cloaks, and dusted the snow from them. Matsuzo rubbed his cold hands. "Now tell me why you insisted on coming here instead of going directly to Ikken's house."

Zenta was looking around the room. At Matsuzo's question he smiled faintly. "The tavern keeper here once did me a favor, and I feel that I owe him something."

Matsuzo was incredulous. "That little man? I don't believe he ever did anyone a favor in his life—unless he got well paid for it."

"Well, he didn't *know* he was doing me a favor," said Zenta. "What happened was this. When I came to this village ten years ago, I was very young, and I had just left home." He paused and then said awkwardly, "I was going through a rather bad time then."

Matsuzo nodded. He knew that his companion had become a ronin under tragic circumstances. It was a topic they avoided.

4

Mastering himself, Zenta continued. "As I sat drinking in this tavern, I wondered whether there was any point in living. I was penniless and couldn't even pay for my drinks. The only thing of value I had was a tiny ivory figurine, very precious, my last link with home. I gave it to the tavern keeper and asked him to sell it for me."

"And he did you a favor by giving you a generous price?" asked Matsuzo.

Zenta laughed harshly. "Not exactly. The tavern keeper saw that I was young and desperate. He told me the figurine was worthless, but he would accept it as payment for my drinks."

"What!"

"Of course there was nothing I could do, since I had no money to pay him. But the sheer gall of the man made me so angry that it shook me out of my gloom and self-pity. Instead of contemplating suicide, I marched off in a fury and went up into the hills here. That was how I met Ikken and became his student."

Matsuzo laughed also. "So that was the favor this miserable wretch did. He saved your life!"

The tavern keeper approached with a tray containing bottles of sake, cups, and small dishes of salted snacks. When he left, Zenta tasted the wine and made a face. "Horrible stuff. He must be saving the good wine for himself. In ten years he hasn't changed a bit."

Matsuzo nodded, hoping that they would soon leave now that Zenta had paid this pilgrimage to the past, although he understood his companion's nostalgia. New Year's was a time for remembering all the childhood delights of the season. A ronin cut off from family ties would long for home at this time of the year. He would remember all the New Year's festivities, the visits, and the gifts from relatives. Matsuzo knew that that was the reason why Zenta, normally careless of his appearance, had saved money to buy new clothes and gifts. The old tea master was his *sensei*, his teacher. More than teacher, he had been almost a father, and for Zenta visiting Ikken was like going home.

Zenta drained his wine cup and put it down without attempting to pour more. "Shall we go?" he asked, picking up his sword.

Before the two ronin could get up, the front door of the tavern slid open. Four men, huge and shapeless in their straw cloaks, entered in a swirl of powdered snow and icy wind. Immediately the tiny room became crowded.

The tavern keeper hurried out at the sound of the door opening. A frightened hiss escaped him when he saw the newcomers, but then his small mouth tightened and his jaw set stubbornly. After he bowed a greeting to the four men, his eyes darted a quick look at the two ronin.

"Where is the money you owe us for the medicine?" asked the man who looked like the leader of the group. "You said you'd have it ready by New Year's Eve." He resembled some kind of forest animal, with his yellow eyes, unkempt hair, and unshaven jowls. The bristling straw cloak he wore added to the resemblance.

Above the odor of the straw Matsuzo smelled something pungent. Then he noticed that one of the men had a back pack consisting of small wooden boxes roped together. From the pack and from the leader's question, Matsuzo realized that the men were medicine peddlers. But he also caught a glimpse of swords under their cloaks. He began to suspect that these tough-looking men were bandits as well as peddlers.

At the speaker's rough tone the tavern keeper had cringed, but now he looked again at the two ronin and seemed to gather courage. "Business has been very bad, sir," he whined. "Please give me a little more time. I will try to pay after New Year's. I promise."

"You have more money than anybody else in this miserable village," said the newcomer, grinning ferociously with his red lips and showing sharp teeth. "You've been cheating your customers long enough."

"I wasn't the one who wanted to buy the medicine in the first place," protested the tavern keeper. "It was my wife. She bought it without asking me. I kept telling her that the Vampire Cat attacked only young girls, but she didn't listen to me and bought the medicine for herself anyway."

The peddler still looked more surprised than angry at the tavern keeper's resistance. "Are you seriously trying to get out of paying? Your stinginess has finally robbed you of your wits!" He took a step toward the tavern keeper, and the latter cringed back but continued to shake his head stubbornly.

Now the peddler was no longer smiling. "People who owe me money soon find out that it's better to pay promptly. You bought the medicine. Now hand over the money."

The tavern keeper retreated until his back was against

the wall. "I won't pay! Your band has terrorized the village long enough! We have no more money left!"

"Just a moment," said Zenta, rising and addressing the medicine peddler. "How much money does he owe you?"

Matsuzo plucked at Zenta's sleeve. "We should keep out of this," he whispered. "You don't really owe the tavern keeper anything."

Ignoring Matsuzo's tug, Zenta pulled out some money. "I'll pay you what he owes," he told the medicine peddler. Then he asked, "What did he mean when he said you were terrorizing the village?"

After Zenta's unexpected assistance, the tavern keeper became bolder. "I'll tell you! There is a story going around that a vampire cat is attacking all the girls in the village. Of course I don't believe a word of it. These peddlers came and claimed to sell a medicine that would keep the cat away. It's just a scheme to frighten the women and children and extort money from helpless people!"

"Liar!" roared the peddler. "Trying to get out of paying your debts, are you? I'll teach you!" He picked up the tavern keeper as if he were a twig broom and with a heave of his powerful shoulders hurled the kicking man against the wall.

The wall consisted of two sliding panels set inside grooves along the top and bottom. Under the impact of the tavern keeper's body, the panels flew out of their grooves and fell flat on the ground, opening the whole side of the house to the back.

Out in the back was the kitchen, where a white-faced woman and a young boy were pounding rice paste in a tub to make New Year's rice cakes. As the tavern keeper hurtled toward them, they dropped their wooden mallets and ran off shrieking.

Up to this point Matsuzo had been determined to stay out of the affair, since the miserly tavern keeper seemed to be getting exactly what he deserved. The man was probably trying to use him and Zenta as a shield in order to get out of paying the peddlers. The incredible story of the Vampire Cat was to make him look like a helpless victim so that the two ronin would come to his aid. Matsuzo wanted no part of the quarrel, and he hoped Zenta wouldn't become involved any further.

At the same time the young ronin was becoming annoyed at the other three medicine peddlers, whose straw cloaks brushed his face as they shifted around in the tiny, crowded room. One of them swung about, knocking over two bottles of sake and spilling the hot wine into Matsuzo's lap. The young ronin jumped to his feet. "Now look here—" he began.

"You stay out of this," ordered one of the peddlers, roughly pushing Matsuzo back. "This is none of your business."

Meanwhile Zenta had gone to the back of the house and was bending over the moaning tavern keeper. The latter clutched Zenta's arm. "Don't let him hurt me any more!"

The intrusion of the ronin further infuriated the leader of the peddlers. He reached out for the nearest weapon, a wooden mallet left by one of the rice cake makers.

Matsuzo saw the motion and cried, "Look out!"

But Zenta had already sensed the threatening move. He straightened quickly and jogged the elbow of the peddler. The latter, reaching for the mallet, missed his aim and instead plunged his arm into the tub of sticky rice paste.

Furious, the powerful peddler picked up the whole tub and swung it at his enemy. It would have been a deadly weapon, but its heavy weight slowed the action down and Zenta had ample time to step aside.

The tub came unstuck from the peddler's arm and fell on the foot of one of the other peddlers. The man screamed. A great deal of the rice paste still stuck to the first peddler's arm. He scraped at it, but it merely passed from one hand to the other and back again. Next he tried flapping his wrists. Only after shaking them violently did he succeed in getting rid of most of it.

From that point the rice paste quickly spread around the room. Some of it landed on the floor, and one of the other peddlers stepped on it. Hopping on one foot, he tried to pull the sticky lump from his boot. Hopping next to him was the peddler nursing his injured foot.

Quantities of the rice paste became mixed up with straw cloaks. A large lump landed on Matsuzo's face, sticking to his eyebrows and covering his eyes. He winced as he pulled at it. "Zenta! I can't get it off!"

Then he heard Zenta's voice say, "Drop your hands and stand still." There were two faint swishes. Matsuzo felt the paste fall from his eyes, and he opened them to see Zenta calmly putting away his sword. Touching his face, Matsuzo found that only a little bit of the paste was left on his lashes.

The room had become very quiet. The only noise came from the man who was holding his sore foot and moaning.

Matsuzo knew that Zenta's intention was to end the fight without bloodshed and that he had chosen this way of demonstrating his skill to discourage the peddlers. He had certainly succeeded. Hostilities forgotten, the tavern keeper and the peddlers simply stood and stared.

Suddenly the tavern keeper burst out laughing hysterically. "You would make a very efficient barber, sir," he told Zenta. "You can shave the customer's face with just two strokes of your sword!"

Matsuzo had no patience left with the tavern keeper. "You impudent scoundrel! It was all your fault that the whole thing started!"

Zenta, too, had had enough of the tavern. "It's time to go," he told Matsuzo. "Let me leave some money here first."

The leader of the medicine peddlers stirred. "I heard your friend call out your name just now," he said, looking hard at the ronin. "Are you Konishi Zenta?"

When Zenta nodded, the peddler said, "I think I've heard about you."

"Then you've probably heard that I don't go around looking for fights," said Zenta.

"Yes, I've heard that, too," said the peddler slowly. He appeared to think for a moment, and when he spoke again his voice was softer, with a certain rough courtesy. "There is no reason why we should become enemies. We won't interfere with your business if you don't interfere with ours."

"I wasn't trying to interfere with your business just now," said Zenta.

The tavern keeper seemed disappointed at the prospect of a truce. "But—but—" he began.

"You be quiet!" said the peddler, spinning fiercely to face him. "The gentleman here paid your debt this time, but next time you might not be so lucky."

Turning back to his men, he said, "Let's go. We've wasted enough time already." At the door he paused and then said in a voice meant to be overheard, "In the future we'll be bringing reinforcements when we go out to collect our debts."

2

Outside, the snow had stopped and the sky was clearing. But the short day was already drawing to a close and the low winter sun tinged the village houses pink, giving them a misleading look of warmth.

The two ronin walked noiselessly, the powdery snow deadening the sound of their steps. Matsuzo looked around but could not see the four medicine peddlers, although there were fresh footsteps pointing in the opposite direction. "What do you think of those peddlers?" he asked his companion. "Are they likely to give us any trouble?"

"They don't have any reason to be angry with *us*," said Zenta. "Nobody was seriously hurt back there, and anyway it wasn't our fault that they got mixed up with the rice paste."

"People aren't always logical about where they put the

blame," said Matsuzo. "And those men looked dangerous."

Zenta nodded. "The leader and possibly two others
looked like ronin. They certainly wore their swords as if
they knew how to use them."

Matsuzo thought over the tavern keeper's words. "It
sounds as if the village is being terrorized by the peddlers.
If the people here have been paying large sums of money
to those bandits, that might account for the miserable
condition of the place."

Zenta walked on thoughtfully. "I doubt the peddlers
are outright bandits. The leader seemed to be collecting
a legitimate debt. Whatever is going on is something
more complicated than just banditry."

With the village behind them they began climbing a
narrow, hilly path. Suddenly Matsuzo had the distinct
feeling that something was following them, but because
of the trees on both sides and constant twists and turns
in the path, he was unable to see very far behind him.
He started each time a clump of snow fell from a pine
bough. Even Zenta seemed unusually tense. Several
times he looked back over his shoulder.

"How far is it to Ikken's house?" asked Matsuzo. The
last feeble rays of the sun disappeared behind the hill
they were climbing, and Matsuzo found the darkened
path treacherous.

"We don't have far to go," said Zenta. "Don't worry."

Nevertheless he quickened his steps. Matsuzo shifted
the pack on his back and hurried to keep up. Suddenly
Zenta stopped. He turned his head and appeared to be
listening hard.

"What is it?" asked Matsuzo.

After listening for a few seconds Zenta shook his head and walked on. Presently he said, "I hope those medicine peddlers don't molest Ikken. In his youth he was a good swordsman, but he must be getting old now. He might not be able to defend himself if that band threatens him."

"Didn't you say that he had a son?" asked Matsuzo.

"Yes, he has a son called Shunken, about five years older than I am," replied Zenta. "If Shunken is living at home, there won't be any worry about safety. But when I was here ten years ago, he was already talking about entering the service of—"

Zenta broke off. He slowly turned around and looked back.

"Something is following us, isn't it?" Matsuzo asked quietly.

"Yes," said Zenta. Again he stood listening hard. Then he said, "I'm going to find out what it is."

"What are you going to do?" asked Matsuzo. "We can't run very fast with these packs on our backs, and it's treacherous underfoot."

Zenta quickly shrugged off his pack. "You stay here and watch our luggage. I know a short cut down this hill, and I'll try to come from behind."

Pushing aside some scrub bamboo, Zenta plunged away from the path into the pine trees. Soon the rustling of his passage died away.

Matsuzo removed the load from his own back and set it down. He flexed his stiff fingers, trying to warm them and loosen them up in case he needed to use his sword.

If their stalker was one of the medicine peddlers with unfriendly intentions, he wanted to be prepared.

It became very quiet. Nevertheless Matsuzo still had the definite impression he was not alone. The warmth from the wine and the exercise of the climb had drained away, leaving him very cold. Suppressing a shudder, he looked around, alert for any sound, any movement. What was Zenta doing? If they delayed much longer, it would be difficult to see their way. Already the thin sliver of the moon stood out sharply in the darkened sky.

Into the still air came a thread of sound. Matsuzo tensed. He didn't think it had been made by a human being. But what animal could it be? Most of them should be in their deep winter sleep.

He heard the sound again. Was it his imagination, or did it seem a little closer? This time it rose a little in pitch and then dipped, almost like a cat's mew. A cat's mew! The tavern keeper's words came into his mind, something about a vampire cat attacking the village girls. Of course it was pure superstition, some nonsense only country people would believe. But that mewing sound really did remind him of a cat.

There it was again! He was certain now that it was getting closer. The mewing was followed by harsh, eager panting. Matsuzo's scalp crawled, for there was something uncanny about the sound.

He began to remember all the stories he had heard about cats and their unusual powers. Occasionally one heard of a cat doing a good deed, like the one who stole gold pieces for his poverty-stricken master, but in most of the stories the cats were cruel and bloodthirsty. Very slowly and quietly Matsuzo eased his sword out of its scabbard.

He remembered the story of a vampire cat who was the vengeful ghost of a woman slain by marauding soldiers. The cat would change into a beautiful woman and lure warriors into her home. When she had lulled their suspicions, she would tear their throats and drink their blood.

Where was Zenta? He seemed to have been gone for a long time.

There was another story about a cat who belonged to the daughter of a nobleman. Day by day the girl became paler and weaker, suffering from fainting spells no doctor could explain. Finally a priest hid himself in her room one night. In the middle of the night, when the household was asleep, the girl's cat, who had been sleeping at her feet, suddenly grew into a giant monster cat and pressed the girl's chest until she gasped for breath.

Other stories came into Matsuzo's mind. There was a cat who lured young girls to a lonely spot, killed them, and then assumed their shapes—

The woods to Matsuzo's right exploded with a violent flurry of movement. He whipped his sword up. Something large and dark bounded away down the steep side of the hill, slithered for a moment, and then disappeared. Matsuzo lowered his sword but quickly raised it again when another figure loomed up.

It was Zenta, and he looked furious. "I nearly caught the thing, whatever it was, but I stumbled over a log and it got away." He brushed the snow from his clothes. "Did you see it?"

"Not very well. It was too dark," said Matsuzo, trying to hide how badly shaken he was. He added, "But I did hear some funny sounds."

The two men looked at each other. Matsuzo noticed a scratch on Zenta's neck slowly oozing blood. "You're hurt! Did that animal attack you?"

Zenta found a piece of paper tissue and dabbed at his neck. "I tripped before I could get close to the thing," he said disgustedly. "This is probably just a scratch from a tree branch."

"That doesn't look like a scratch made by a tree branch," Matsuzo said slowly. "Something with a pretty sharp point did that." He swallowed. If the cut had been just a little deeper, it would have been fatal.

Zenta still looked annoyed with himself. "Forget about the scratch. It's already stopped bleeding." He picked up his pack. "Come on, we'd better hurry."

He set a rapid pace up the hill, for the prospect of being outside in complete darkness was unthinkable. Zenta seemed to remember the way and went confidently. Presently he asked, "What kind of funny sound did you hear?"

Matsuzo hesitated. Now that he was back in Zenta's company, his recent fears seemed foolish. "You won't believe me," he said, "but I thought I heard a catlike mewing."

"So you heard it too!"

"It . . . it wasn't really a cat, was it?" asked Matsuzo.

Zenta shook his head. "No. It was much too big."

That had been Matsuzo's impression, too. "It was certainly too big for a normal house cat."

"Well, we don't have tigers in this country," said Zenta. "Only in paintings, and besides, they don't mew —they roar."

Tigers, vampire cats, they occurred only in paintings and folk tales, thought Matsuzo, not in real life. Nevertheless he couldn't keep from continually looking back over his shoulder as they walked.

He was relieved when he heard Zenta's voice say, "Here we are. That's Ikken's house just ahead."

Matsuzo had worried that the old tea master might have died or moved away. But somebody, at least, was at home, for he could hear voices from behind the closed front gate. One was a woman's voice and it sounded annoyed.

The two men stopped at the gate and removed their packs. Just as Zenta was about to knock on the gate, it opened and two figures appeared. One of them, a woman, was carrying a lantern, and behind her was a young girl. Both were dressed for the outdoors in cloaks and cloth hoods.

They must have been startled at the unexpected sight of two strange men, for the girl gave a little scream.

There was an angry growl and something launched itself at Matsuzo, knocking him to the ground. The breath of some beast was hot on his face. Remembering the mewing sounds he had heard earlier, he felt a flash of pure panic.

Behind him Matsuzo heard the hiss of Zenta's sword whipping out of its sheath. But already Matsuzo saw the gaping jaws and flashing teeth just inches from his nose. Frantically thrusting his arms over his face, he expected the sharp teeth to sink into his throat any moment. It took him a few seconds to realize that the animal was not trying to tear him to pieces, but was only pinning him down.

"Put away your sword," said a woman's voice. "Asa, call off your animal."

"Yes, Mother," said a girl's voice. "Down, Kongomaru!"

The weight lifted from Matsuzo's chest. He slowly got to his feet, brushed the snow from his back, and examined his assailant. It was a large dog.

The girl, Asa, who was evidently the dog's mistress, peered anxiously at Matsuzo. "Kongomaru hasn't hurt you, has he?"

The young ronin shook his head, too astonished to speak. Asa petted her dog. "He really is a good-natured dog, only a little playful at times."

At Asa's words Kongomaru gave every sign of living up to his mistress's recommendation. He sat down, thumped his tail a few times, and panted good-naturedly. But one of his ears was torn, a sign that he was no stranger to fights. He was of a breed called *akita-inu*, native to the region and known for its toughness and intelligence. His muzzle and the tips of his ears were black, but the rest of him was white, except for a large tan-colored patch on his back and neck. Altogether he was a fine-looking, powerful dog.

Zenta put away his sword. "What fun you must have with Kongomaru," he said to the girl. "Does he knock you down, too, or is that just a game with strangers?"

"Kongomaru never knocks people down!" cried Asa.

On seeing Zenta's smile she added, "Well, only rarely. If you put your hand out to him, he'll make friends with you, I promise."

Matsuzo had his doubts, but Zenta was already putting out his hand, though cautiously. Kongomaru, after a look at his mistress, thumped his tail and allowed his head to be patted.

Feeling it shameful not to follow Zenta's example, Matsuzo reached out and patted Kongomaru gingerly. When that was well received, he went a step further and scratched the dog's ear. Kongomaru sniffed Matsuzo's hand. "He really is a nice dog," said the young ronin, surprised. "I wonder why he jumped on me at first."

"He attacked you because my daughter screamed," said the mother curtly. "We've trained him to protect her."

"Then you feel that a protector is needed around here?" asked Zenta.

"Since we don't have your showy methods of defense, we have to resort to dogs." The woman's eyes were on Zenta's swords as she spoke. In the light from her lantern, her face looked sardonic.

Matsuzo stared at her in surprise. Her tone was hostile. He saw no reason for her attitude: if anything, *he* was the injured party.

The girl, Asa, looked more friendly. "Are you coming to visit my uncle?" she asked.

"Your uncle?" exclaimed Zenta. He turned to the girl's mother. "Then you are Ikken's sister?"

"He is my brother-in-law," said the woman. "I married his younger brother, and we moved to this village five years ago. We stayed on after my husband died."

"I don't remember Ikken mentioning his brother," said Zenta.

The woman's mouth twisted bitterly. "Of course Ikken wouldn't mention him. He felt that his brother had disgraced his family by marrying a woman from the merchant class."

"Why is it a disgrace?" asked Zenta. "Many samurai marry women from the merchant class, and their wives become samurai women."

"Ah, but it was different in my husband's case," said the woman. "When we married, my husband was adopted by my father to inherit his business. My father is only a lowly merchant, but he is wealthy. My husband had grown tired of being a penniless ronin, and he was glad to exchange his precious family name for our money."

The girl, Asa, seemed embarrassed by her mother's words. "Come, Mother. These gentlemen seem to be Uncle Ikken's friends, and they don't like to hear you talk this way."

At the girl's words Matsuzo peered at her more closely and found that she was not so young as he had thought at first. Her words suggested maturity, and he decided that she was perhaps sixteen or even older. Her voice sounded well-bred, attractive, and friendly, but her features were hard to determine in the poor light. Matsuzo decided that he would try to meet her again at the earliest opportunity for a better look.

The girl's mother seemed less hostile and for the first

time showed a little curiosity about the two ronin. "Are you friends or relatives of Ikken?" she asked.

"He was my teacher many years ago," replied Zenta. "I've come to pay my respects to him."

"You haven't been back for a long time, then?"

"No, not for nearly ten years. I hope Ikken is in good health?"

When there was no immediate answer Zenta said quickly, "Is he sick?"

"No, Ikken isn't sick, but you'll find things very changed here," said the woman heavily. After a moment she said, "I'm sorry for Kongomaru's behavior. Perhaps you can forgive us and visit us at our house."

Matsuzo had the impression that she was about to say something else. He welcomed her friendlier attitude and her invitation, however. "Do you live far from here?" he asked.

"No, our house is down that hill, closer to the village," replied the woman. Turning to her daughter, she said, "We'd better hurry home, Asa. It's getting late."

Matsuzo suddenly realized that the women would have to pass by the place where they had had the terrifying encounter with the strange animal. "It's not safe for you to go alone," he said. "We'll come with you."

"I know it's not safe," the mother snapped. Some of her earlier hostility seemed to have returned. "But we commoners have no need for your swordsmanship. Kongomaru is enough protection for us."

Zenta spoke up. "I'm sure Kongomaru will protect you from people like us. But when we were coming up here, we nearly had a struggle with some dangerous creature that was making strange mewing noises. Are you sure Kongomaru would be a match for that?"

"Oh, Mother, it was the Cat!" cried the girl, shrinking against her mother and clutching her arm.

Matsuzo had been petting Kongomaru, who was showing further signs of becoming friendly. But at the mention of the Cat, the dog tensed and growled. Matsuzo could feel the hair rise on the dog's back.

"Of course it's the Cat," said the mother coolly. "And what better protector than a big dog? Pull yourself together, Asa. We have to hurry home."

After bowing to the two ronin, the mother and daughter turned and walked away, followed by the big dog, Kongomaru.

Soon the light from their lantern disappeared behind a hill. Matsuzo was still uneasy. "Are you sure we should let them go off by themselves?"

"If they don't want us, we can't force ourselves on them," said Zenta. "The mother seems to think that with Kongomaru's protection, they will be quite safe."

"Yes, but even she believed in the Cat. And she didn't strike me as a person who imagined things." Matsuzo remembered the woman's calm, cool manner. He didn't like her, but he couldn't help admiring her courage.

"After our own experience," said Zenta, "we know that the Cat is more than just a story made up by the peddlers to frighten the villagers. Whatever that animal was back there, it was unfriendly."

"Yes," Matsuzo agreed soberly. "And it mewed."

3

"Why doesn't someone answer?" said Zenta. "Those two women have only just left. The household can't be fast asleep already."

Matsuzo sighed. "If they're retired for the night, we'll have to trudge all the way back to the village. I don't relish the thought."

Just as Zenta was about to give up and turn away, he noticed something strange. The gate was slightly ajar. "What can the gatekeeper be thinking of!" he said. "He didn't bar the gate after the two women left! And he doesn't answer when I call. Where is he, anyway?"

Footsteps, shuffling and slow, finally approached. "Who is there?" asked a voice. It sounded irritable.

The voice was familiar, thought Zenta. Perhaps it was one of the servants he had known before. "My name is Konishi Zenta," he announced. "I studied with your master ten years ago, and I have come with a friend to pay my respects."

For some time there was no answer from the other side of the gate. Zenta could hear Matsuzo impatiently stamping his feet, trying to keep warm. Perhaps the old servant was deaf? Zenta raised his voice. "My name is—"

"Yes, yes, I heard you the first time! Konishi Zenta . . . I remember now."

Slowly the gate opened wide. In the near darkness Zenta saw an old man, rather stooped. But before he could get a good look, the man turned and walked across the courtyard, saying over his shoulder, "Come along. Hurry up, it's late."

The two ronin looked at each other in amazement before hurrying to obey. The crusty old man was certainly a strange servant. Zenta wondered why Ikken kept him—but, then, one could not dismiss a retainer grown old in one's service.

Lengthening his stride, Zenta caught up to the old man and said, "Before we see your master, can we take these bundles to the kitchen and hand them over to the cook? We brought some food and wine with us."

The old man, who had stopped at the edge of the veranda to remove his clogs, paused and gave a little snort that sounded like a laugh. "Very well, come this way."

The two ronin sat on the front veranda of the house and pulled off their boots. Then they entered the house and followed the old man down a dark corridor, their damp feet squeaking slightly on the ice-cold wooden floor. At the end of the corridor the old man pushed open a sliding door.

Zenta followed him into a room almost totally dark, but he guessed that it was the kitchen from the unmistakable smell of soy sauce and bean paste. He heard a flint being struck, and in a moment there was a faint illumination as a wick caught fire in a dish of oil.

In the light of this tiny lamp Zenta examined the face of the old man. The realization hit him like a blow. He stared aghast at the high, narrow forehead, the hollow cheeks, and the thin, sensitive lips, features he could never forget. He sank to his knees. "Please forgive me, Sensei," he managed to say. "I didn't recognize you!"

Ikken, the tea master, cleared his throat gruffly. "Well, well, never mind. Your mistake was natural. I'm alone, you see, and there is no gatekeeper."

"Alone!" cried Zenta. "There is no one else living here at all?" It was only then that he noticed the room had none of the normal kitchen clutter. On the table next to the lamp he saw a tray containing one rice bowl, one soup bowl, one pickle dish, and one pair of chopsticks. Looking at this pathetic evidence of Ikken's loneliness, Zenta felt his throat tighten. "Where is Shunken?" he asked at last.

Ikken made no reply, and Zenta thought for a moment that he had not heard the question. The tea master's face was fixed in a faint smile, like some exquisitely carved Buddhist saint in a temple. Then the smile dissolved and Ikken moved away, groping for the flint to light another lamp. He spoke in a voice so low that Zenta had to strain to catch the words. "Shunken is dead. He was killed in battle three years ago."

For a few moments Ikken gave his whole attention to trimming the wick of the lamp. When he spoke again his voice sounded normal. "You must be hungry. You'll have to eat the food you brought yourself, I'm afraid, since there is not much here."

Zenta gave a guilty start. "We don't have to eat anything now," he protested.

"Nonsense," said Ikken. "Young men like you have hearty appetites. After eating, you know where to find a place to sleep. The bedding probably needs to be aired, but there are plenty of quilts."

"I'm sorry to give you trouble," said Zenta. "If I had known—"

"Don't be sorry," said Ikken. For the first time he looked at Zenta as if really seeing him. "I'm glad that you've come. After you've eaten come into my room and we'll have tea."

As the door closed behind Ikken, Zenta turned to Matsuzo and found his companion looking rather dazed. It was probably the result of surprise, fatigue, and hunger. Untying his pack and opening some boxes of food, he said, "I had no idea that Ikken had been reduced to living like this. No wonder the sister-in-law said things were changed here. If her family is so rich, why doesn't she try to help out a little?"

The fire in the wood stove was not completely out, and Matsuzo began fanning it to flames. He said, "It's quite likely that Ikken is too proud to accept any help. The daughter certainly looked friendly and affectionate enough."

Zenta smiled to himself. Matsuzo had an eye for pretty girls, and in every town they had visited there was probably a girl sighing or shedding a few tears of regret.

"If you want to see Asa and her mother again, we can visit them tomorrow morning," said Zenta. "Maybe we can find out more about this cat business, too."

"I'd like to see that dog Kongomaru again," said Matsuzo eagerly. "Imagine coming to his mistress's defense like that!"

Searching around the kitchen, Zenta found a pan of watery soup made from seaweed. He tried it and found it almost tasteless, but since the food they brought was cold, any hot liquid would be welcome. He didn't mind the snow or the bitter wind outside, but the darkness and desolation of Ikken's house chilled him to the bone. He rummaged in the cupboards until he found another soup bowl. The dishes were thick with dust from months, or even years, of neglect.

As he sipped his soup and ate, Zenta reflected that he had never seen the kitchen before, although he had stayed nearly a year with Ikken. In those days Ikken had a dozen servants. Although a ronin, he was well off, for he had saved some money and valuables, and his fame as a tea master had brought him the patronage of powerful warlords. Now his son was dead and his servants all had deserted him.

Zenta remembered vividly his first meeting with the tea master. He had just been cheated by the tavern keeper, and as he left the village and strode up the hillside, his anger gradually turned to loathing—for himself and for the whole world.

Halfway up the hill he met Ikken, who was standing motionless, contemplating a rock. When Zenta would have walked past without a word, Ikken politely invited him to join in admiring the rock. Unhurriedly, he pointed out the beauty of the rock: its shape, its texture, and the color of the lichen mottling its surface.

Apparently Ikken had seen Zenta coming from a distance and had sensed his desperation. In a quiet, firm voice Ikken proceeded to calm him the way he would a wild dog or cat. And in the end, Zenta followed the tea master home like a stray.

He stayed on and studied with Ikken, learning concentration, self-control, and serenity. The tea master's son, Shunken, was living at home then. Five years older than Zenta and ambitious for glory, he was impatient to leave the small village where his father had chosen to make his home. Shunken was already a brilliant swordsman, and he taught Zenta a great deal during their violent practice sessions together.

There was a clatter, and Zenta woke from his reverie with a start. Matsuzo was collecting the soup bowls. "I'd better wash these, since Ikken has no servants to help him. Can you tell me where I can get some water?"

Zenta got up and stretched. "It's too cold for washing dishes. Let's put them away in that cupboard and do them tomorrow."

"All right," agreed Matsuzo readily. He yawned. "Where shall we sleep?"

"We can sleep in the room I used to have. I'm going to Ikken's study for tea, but you can find the room if you go down that corridor and turn right. It's the second door. There will probably be plenty of bedding on the shelves."

On the way to the tea master's study, Zenta stopped at a door that opened to a small courtyard with a stone basin. It was used for a ritual rinsing of the mouth and hands before a tea ceremony. Zenta found the water in the basin frozen hard, but there was a bucket of fresh water standing on the ground, thoughtfully placed there by the tea master. The cold water made Zenta's hands ache, but the ritual of washing began to purify him of his fatigue and agitation.

In front of Ikken's study Zenta knelt down and pushed open the door slightly. "Sensei, may I come in?"

"Yes, come in," said Ikken. "The fire is ready. While the water heats we can talk. I want to hear what you have been doing since you left here."

Seeing Ikken seated once more at his familiar place in the study, Zenta felt that the tea master was not as aged as he had thought at first. True, he had many more lines in his face and his hair was now mostly gray, but in repose he regained his old dignity and was no longer the stooped, shambling figure whose appearance had shocked Zenta so much.

Ikken smiled with genuine warmth. "So. Konishi Zenta—I remember picking that name for you. Now tell me about yourself."

Ten years was a long time, and Zenta described only the few turning points in his life. Ikken was one of the few people who knew the full story of his family background and a person to whom he could confide his doubts about his actions and his decisions.

Ikken nodded occasionally as Zenta talked, and at the end he said, "You have matured and grown strong. I'm glad to see that you have made peace with yourself. I knew that when you had regained your self-respect, you'd come back to visit me. I approve of what I see. You have turned out well."

The tea master's approval meant more to Zenta than praise from a powerful warlord. He bowed his head, deeply moved. When he looked up he saw that Ikken's eyes were closed and his lips tight with grief. Zenta guessed that the tea master was thinking of his son, Shunken.

Suddenly Ikken shook himself. "But I'm forgetting about the tea. It's been a long time since I've performed the tea ceremony."

Zenta remembered his gift. Reaching behind him, he brought out a small wooden box and pushed it toward the tea master. "Please overlook my lack of taste and accept this poor gift."

Ikken untied the ribbon around the box and removed the cover. He lifted the clay bowl from the box, turning it slowly to examine it in the light. The bowl was squat in shape, with an irregular rim, and in the lamp light the reddish brown surface glowed here and there with coppery tints. "A Bizen bowl," murmured Ikken. "We'll use it now."

Watching Ikken's fingers caressing the bowl, Zenta knew that the price he had paid for the bowl, the months of galling work and humiliation, had not been too high.

Tea had been brought to Japan from China, and at first it was used only as a medicine. Later, Zen Buddhists used the drink to clear the mind and help promote meditation. Even after the drink was taken up by the nobility and the samurai, tea still retained its associations with Zen Buddhism, and most of the great tea masters studied Zen. For the samurai, the tea ceremony was a temporary escape from their violent world into tranquility.

The warrior class admired the mental discipline and self-control necessary in the tea ceremony. Great warlords made a point of honoring the tea masters, even employing them on important missions. But some tea masters disliked the richness of the tea rooms in the castles of the wealthy feudal lords. Many, like Ikken, preferred to live in seclusion and perform their tea ceremony in an atmosphere of rustic simplicity, which they felt was truer to the spirit of tea.

Zenta followed Ikken to the corner of the study that was screened off as a tea room. As he looked around he realized that the stark decor there showed more than rustic simplicity; it revealed poverty. The alcove that usually displayed a valuable painting, scroll, or vase showed only a clay jar with a single sprig of plum blossom. The shelf containing tea utensils was almost bare. Of Ikken's three fine bamboo whisks, Zenta could see only one. There was no sign of Ikken's priceless tea caddy, and instead of the valuable ceramic water jar that he remembered, Zenta saw only a bamboo bucket. Even the iron kettle sitting on the hearth was a coarse one made by some village craftsman.

If Ikken noticed Zenta's surprise at the disappearance of his valuables, he gave no sign of it. Zenta was ashamed of his preoccupation with the lost utensils and set himself to enjoy what there was to see in the tea room. The rough texture of the clay flower jar echoed the bark of the plum branch. In the sunken hearth the ashes had been beautifully molded, even sculptured. Ikken had arranged some pieces of charcoal with exquisite care.

Zenta now recalled that Ikken made his own charcoal. He had even helped the tea master fire the pieces of specially aged hardwood in an oven at the back of the house. Ikken was a perfectionist about using charcoal of great purity. He used to say that charcoal with impurities would give off an odor, which would clash with the fragrance of the tea or of the incense.

It was the incense that brought back Zenta's memories most vividly, for this particular incense had been Shunken's favorite. But the valuable porcelain incense burner was gone with the rest of Ikken's utensils, and the incense now burned in the hot ashes of the hearth.

Ikken's motions were as careful and controlled as if he still handled his precious utensils. Zenta had seen tea ceremonies performed in the households of warlords eager to demonstrate their culture. But there, the anxiety to do everything correctly produced tense and ugly movements. Ikken, on the other hand, moved smoothly and confidently, doing everything right without worrying about being correct.

He took a small bamboo scoop and measured powdered

tea into the Bizen bowl, afterward wiping the scoop with a small piece of silk cloth. Picking up the bamboo ladle so that its handle made just the proper angle with his wrist, he added hot water to the bowl. The motion he made in setting down the ladle back on the kettle was as beautiful and economical as that of a swordsman sheathing his sword. He picked up the bamboo whisk and whipped the tea until it became foamy. Then he offered the bowl to his guest.

Zenta picked up the bowl with both hands and drank the foamy tea in three and a half sips. As the bittersweet, astringent taste spread over his tongue, he felt more peaceful than he had for years. He was soothed not so much by the drink itself as by the utter rightness of everything Ikken had done.

Zenta returned the bowl, murmuring his thanks. After Ikken rinsed and wiped the bowl and replaced the utensils, the two men returned to the main part of the study. For a while they sat silent, savoring the contentment brought by the tea ceremony.

Finally Ikken broke the silence and said, "You have chosen a life that will not bring you wealth or rank. Perhaps the training in frugality provided by the tea ceremony was a good thing for you."

"Do you think my unsettled way of life is too aimless?" asked Zenta.

"Being unsettled and being aimless are different," replied Ikken. "Going from place to place helping people in trouble is a very worthy aim."

The mention of people in trouble reminded Zenta of the medicine peddlers. "I met some rather rough men in the village today," he began. "They claimed to sell a medicine that would ward off cats—" He stopped when he saw the expression on Ikken's face.

The tea master was staring at the scratch on Zenta's neck, his eyes wide with fear. "You'd better wash that scratch before it turns angry," he said shakily.

"It's nothing," protested Zenta.

But the peace and contentment of the tea ceremony had been shattered. Ikken suddenly put his hands over his eyes. "It's late, and I'm rather tired," he muttered. It was a dismissal.

As Zenta made his bow and left the room, he felt deeply disturbed. Ikken must also be a victim of the medicine peddlers' extortion. That would explain the disappearance of the tea utensils and other household valuables. Perhaps Ikken's servants had deserted him because he could no longer support them.

Zenta found his old room and pushed open the door. Matsuzo was under a huge mound of quilts, as if sheer weight might push out the cold. At Zenta's entrance, he grunted a greeting and then pulled his head further into the mound until only his topknot was showing.

Zenta unfolded a mattress and spread it out on the ground. The mattress smelled musty and was slightly damp. Well, he had slept in conditions just as bad and expected to sleep in far worse conditions in the future.

As he pulled the quilts up to his chin, Zenta thought about what possible hold the medicine peddlers could have on Ikken. The tea master could not be afraid for his life, since he was a ronin and trained to a samurai's indifference to death. Then Zenta remembered the tavern keeper's words. The peddlers sold medicine to people whose daughters were menaced by a vampire cat. Ikken had no daughter, but he had a niece, the girl Asa. Although the sister-in-law was an unfriendly woman, the girl had spoken of her uncle with affection. With Shunken dead, she was Ikken's only surviving blood relation.

4

In spite of his exhaustion Matsuzo's sleep was fitful. Horrible dreams kept him tossing and turning. A monstrous animal knocked him to the ground and pinned him down, its weight on his chest preventing him from breathing. The monster opened its wide tiger jaws, but only thin mewing sounds came out. It wasn't a tiger after all; it was a cat with yellow, glowing eyes. No, it wasn't a cat; it was the dog Kongomaru. But for some reason the dog had turned vicious and was not responding to his mistress's voice. And Asa's voice had changed grotesquely and was now as deep as a man's.

It was Zenta calling to him. "You have too many quilts on. No wonder you're restless. How can you sleep with so much weight on your chest?"

After removing two of his quilts Matsuzo slept more easily, although he was not completely free of his nightmares. The medicine peddlers were really animals pretending to be human. The straw cloaks they wore turned into fur and soon, dropping their pretense, they went down on all fours. One of them was licking himself like a cat, trying to get rid of the rice paste stuck on his fur. In the background the tavern keeper was laughing like a madman, making thin, keening noises.

Matsuzo sat up groaning. There was no use trying to sleep any longer. He saw that the pale winter morning light was showing through the papered door and that Zenta was already up and gone. Matsuzo got up creakily and immediately went about working the stiffness from his joints. No samurai could afford to be in this terrible state.

After a wash with some stinging cold water from the garden well, Matsuzo felt much better, exhilarated in fact. He was also very hungry. In the kitchen he found Zenta seated before a pile of food boxes eating his breakfast. He looked rather wan.

"You didn't sleep very well either?" asked Matsuzo.

"No," admitted Zenta. "Our meeting with that cat creature must have bothered me. I kept having nightmares about the thing."

"That's funny, I dreamt about the cat, too," Matsuzo said. "And I thought it was because I had too many covers on."

He took up some of the food boxes and was surprised to see that several of them were already empty. Surely Zenta couldn't have eaten all that by himself?

Zenta noticed his surprise. "Ikken helped himself to

the food before I got up. After all, we brought these things for him, didn't we?"

Knowing that Zenta was sensitive about his teacher's poverty, Matsuzo hastily changed the subject. "What do you think we should do about the monstrous cat? We can't let the village continue to be terrorized. That girl, Asa, might really be in danger."

Zenta nodded. "The sooner we do something, the better. I'm positive that Ikken is one of the people victimized. All his valuables must have been sold to pay for protection against the cat."

From what he could see of the tea master's house, Matsuzo found that easy to believe. In the merciless daylight the signs of poverty and neglect were even more obvious. The floorboards were loose in many places, and the doors of several cupboards were split and warped. Even the eating utensils in the kitchen were coarse, wooden ware normally used by peasants, not the fine lacquered ware they would expect to find in the home of someone like Ikken.

Between mouthfuls of cold black beans Matsuzo said, "Perhaps we can ask Ikken how many men there are in that band of medicine peddlers. If there are not too many of them, the two of us might be able to drive them away from the region."

"It's not so simple as that," said Zenta. He was warming his hands around a bowl of seaweed soup left over from the previous night and reheated. "I don't want to bring up the subject with Ikken. He was a warrior when he was young, and his son Shunken a notable swordsman. To admit that he was frightened into pay-

ing the medicine peddlers would be too humiliating for
Ikken."

Matsuzo saw Zenta's point. But in order to fight the
enemy, they needed information. "I can visit Asa and
her mother," he said, brightening. "They will be able to
tell me about the cat menace."

"That's a good idea," said Zenta. "Meanwhile I can
go back to the tavern keeper. He must know everything
that happens in this village, and I can find out more
about the band of medicine peddlers."

He rose and began to gather up the dirty dishes. "I
suppose we should try to wash these."

"Let's put them away in the cupboard with last night's
dishes," suggested Matsuzo. They could always wash the
dishes when they had more time. The shelves were still
full of dishes they hadn't used yet.

After breakfast, Matsuzo lost no time setting out for
Asa's house.

Outside, the snow sparkled in the sunlight with a hard
brilliance that hurt the eyes. He took a deep breath and
coughed a little from the cold, but he felt good. He
suddenly realized that it was New Year's Day. At home
this had always been a day of furious activity, paying
visits to the shrine, making formal calls on superiors, and
receiving calls from inferiors. So much had happened
that they had completely forgotten the day!

He walked down the mountain path, enjoying the
crisp crunch of the snow underfoot. In the daylight the
trees on either side of the path seemed less densely
packed. Everything looked so pleasant and normal that

he felt ashamed of his nervousness the previous night. But the catlike thing that had stalked them was not a product of his imagination. Zenta had seen it also and had nearly touched it.

Matsuzo tried to remember where the encounter had taken place. It was just beyond that sharp bend in the path, if his memory served him. Yes, he could see the square depressions in the snow where they had rested their packs. He carefully scrutinized the ground beyond the path, hoping to find prints: footprints, paw prints, anything that would give a clue to the nature of the beast. But the snow was so badly churned that black dirt showed and he could see nothing helpful.

Nothing, that is, except a small piece of black cloth caught on the jagged end of a log. Matsuzo picked up the scrap and examined it carefully. The cloth had not come from his clothing or Zenta's, for it was the wrong color. It couldn't have been left by one of the villagers earlier, for it had been snowing most of the day and the scrap would therefore have been covered. The two women had also passed this way, and Matsuzo tried to recall what they wore. The girl Asa had on something brightly colored, and her mother wore something darker, but definitely not black. Matsuzo looked again at the scrap of black cloth. It must have been torn from the clothing of the beast who had been stalking them!

But beasts didn't wear clothes, and therefore it had been a human being. Matsuzo took a deep breath. Someone had been making those mewing noises and pretending to be a cat to frighten people. He was surprised that a whole village had been taken in by such a cheap trick.

Even the tea master, Ikken, had been fooled, and he looked far from stupid.

Looking at the cloth Matsuzo could see nothing remarkable about it. The color and weaving were quite common, of a sort worn by farmers, artisans, and even ronin. He noticed a faint smell that seemed to recall something, but the memory escaped him. Perhaps it came from one of the quack medicines peddled by that unscrupulous band. Zenta might be able to deduce something from the scrap, thought Matsuzo, and tucked it into his sleeve.

Finding Asa's house was not difficult in the daytime. Remembering that the girl's mother had said they were wealthy, Matsuzo went to a large and prosperous-looking house a short distance beyond the village. His guess was confirmed by the sight of a dog's paw prints leading to the front gate. Kongomaru had passed this way.

The house was surrounded by a high, stoutly built wall, more suited to a samurai's mansion than a merchant's country house. Of course Asa's father had been a ronin. Perhaps he had been trying to keep up his former state. On either side of the sturdy front gate were two pine trees, the traditional New Year's decoration. The pine trees denoted long life, and behind each tree were arranged three stalks of bamboo, which symbolized constancy and virtue. Across the top of the gate was a fringed straw rope strung with pieces of folded white paper. Looking at the handsome, elaborate decorations, Matsuzo felt even more keenly the shabbiness of Ikken's house, which didn't show any observance of the New Year season.

The main gate of the house was open, ready to receive the stream of visitors who would be making New Year's calls. Matsuzo went up to the gatekeeper and gave his name, adding that he had met the mistress and her daughter on the previous night.

The gatekeeper bowed very low and invited him in. Stepping across the front courtyard, Matsuzo saw Asa on the front veranda bowing out some visitors. On seeing Matsuzo she broke into a warm smile of welcome. Seated next to her was Kongomaru, his hair sleek and his black ears intelligently cocked.

The girl in her richly colored New Year's kimono was a beautiful sight, but Matsuzo was almost equally delighted to see the dog. He had become very fond of Asa's loyal and courageous protector. In his sleeve Matsuzo carried a little packet of rice balls flavored with fish scraps, his New Year's gift to Kongomaru.

During the exchange of New Year's greetings, Matsuzo saw that his earlier impression of Asa had been correct. The girl's manners were refined and her movements graceful. She had fine, delicate features, with a high, narrow forehead that recalled her uncle, Ikken. But her mouth was different. The lips were full and red.

When the polite greetings were over, Matsuzo reached into his sleeve for the packet of rice balls. Kongomaru instantly sat up and sniffed. With a growl he suddenly launched himself from the veranda straight at Matsuzo, knocking him flat. The young ronin's head hit the ground hard, and for a moment things turned dark. He thought confusedly that time had turned back to the previous night, when Kongomaru had first attacked him.

In the distance the girl's voice was crying something, and when Matsuzo's eyes cleared he saw that Asa was desperately pulling Kongomaru back. Other people appeared in the front courtyard, and the dog was finally dragged away.

Matsuzo struggled to his feet. Not only was he shaken by the fall, but his feelings were deeply hurt as well. He had thought that he had made friends with Kongomaru. What made the dog turn vicious again?

Asa was looking anxiously at him. "Are you hurt? That was a terribly hard fall!"

Matsuzo rubbed the back of his head and felt a lump rising. "I'll be all right in a moment. I guess Kongomaru doesn't like me as much as I thought."

"I don't understand it!" said Asa. "After last night Kongomaru should have known that you were a friend. He is very intelligent, and his instinct is usually extremely good about these things."

"Perhaps *you* had better give him this, then," said Matsuzo ruefully, pulling out his packet of flattened rice balls. "I don't think I'll risk approaching him again."

When Matsuzo pulled out the packet, the piece of black cloth fluttered to the ground. Kongomaru leaped from the hands of the servants. But instead of attacking Matsuzo again, he jumped on the piece of cloth. Seizing it with his teeth, he shook it furiously.

"Why, that's the piece of cloth I found in the woods just now!" cried Matsuzo.

Asa finally succeeded in calming Kongomaru, who, after tearing the cloth to shreds, seemed to feel that his duty was done. He sat down on his haunches, looking pleased with himself, and allowed his mistress to quiet him.

A great light dawned on Matsuzo. "Then Kongomaru wasn't attacking me at all! He was attacking that piece of cloth because he knew it came from someone threatening."

Kongomaru thumped his tail, as if in agreement, and Matsuzo looked at him in admiration. What a brave and intelligent animal! He would give anything to have a dog like this as a faithful companion.

One of the sliding doors facing the veranda opened and Asa's mother appeared, accompanied by a man dressed in the style of a prosperous merchant. Despite Matsuzo's dislike of the woman, he approved of her costume. She was dressed in the dark colors suitable for a widow, but the materials were rich and rustled with the heavy swish of the most expensive silk.

"Asa, what's the meaning of this uproar?" asked the mother.

Asa looked defensive. "Kongomaru made a mistake and jumped at our visitor here."

Kongomaru seemed to realize that he was in disgrace. He crawled away and tried to hide behind his mistress's slender back.

"That dog is hopeless," said the merchant. He turned to Asa's mother and said, "If he doesn't learn better manners soon, you'll have to get rid of him, Toshi."

Matsuzo was torn between indignation on Kongomaru's behalf and surprise at the merchant's tone. The man acted as if he was the head of the house. His round face, with its red cheeks and broad nose, suggested simple good nature. But his eyes did not match the rest of his face. The lids, droopy at the outer corners, gave him a shrewd and cynical look.

Toshi, Asa's mother, said impatiently, "Oh, leave the dog alone, Hirobei. He's just a little too eager to protect Asa from enemies."

"I don't think the stupid beast even knows the difference between friend and enemy," said the merchant Hirobei. Kongomaru's torn ear showed for an instant from behind Asa's back, and they heard a soft whimper.

Matsuzo hastened to defend Kongomaru's good character and presented his theory about the scrap of cloth. The merchant smiled contemptuously. "An interesting theory, but far-fetched, don't you think? I've known Kongomaru longer than you have, and I don't have great hopes for his intelligence. It was a silly idea of Asa's to get him in the first place."

"It wasn't my idea! It was Uncle Ikken's!" cried Asa hotly, kneeling down and putting her arms around Kongomaru's neck. She seemed on the verge of tears.

"Calm yourself, Asa," said her mother. "We're not about to send Kongomaru away. But even your Uncle Ikken doesn't allow Kongomaru inside his front gate."

Matsuzo now remembered that when he and Zenta arrived at Ikken's house, they had seen only the two women emerge from the front gate. Kongomaru must have been waiting outside. "Why doesn't Ikken let Kongomaru into his courtyard, at least?" he asked.

At this question Asa blushed a bright pink. Hirobei laughed. "Asa is too embarrassed, but I'll tell you. Kongomaru once committed a nuisance over Ikken's prized bonsai pine tree, and he has been exiled from the tea master's house ever since!"

"Enough of this nonsense about Kongomaru," said Toshi. Turning to Matsuzo she said, "It's too kind of you to excuse our dog. Can you forgive us and accept some of our New Year's food?"

"You'd better get the maids to brush the gentleman's clothes, Asa," said Hirobei. "We must not let a proper young samurai like this leave with a bad impression of us."

Matsuzo couldn't decide what he disliked most about Hirobei, the man's insults to Kongomaru, his officious meddling in running Toshi's house, or the unctuous politeness he showed toward him, so overdone that it was almost insolent.

When Toshi left to give orders to the servants, followed by the bustling Hirobei, Matsuzo asked Asa, "Is that man really your uncle? Your mother's brother?"

"No, he is only my mother's cousin," replied Asa, scratching Kongomaru's ear fondly, as if to make up for Hirobei's unkindness. "I call him uncle as a courtesy title. He's been managing the family business since my father died. In fact he was manager even earlier—my father didn't take much interest in business."

Matsuzo could understand that. Asa's father, the brother of the tea master, Ikken, came from a samurai family and probably had little skill in business matters. Hirobei looked as if he had all too much skill.

Matsuzo unwrapped his packet of rice balls and held them out to Kongomaru. The rice balls disappeared as if by magic. The dog beamed at Matsuzo and wagged his tail, showing no trace of his former hostility.

"You're trying to thank me, aren't you, Kongomaru?" said the young ronin fondly. "You're not stupid. That nasty man Hirobei doesn't understand you." He looked up and caught a smile on Asa's face. "I know I sound silly," he admitted. "But I've always wanted to have a dog like this, and Kongomaru is unusually intelligent."

"He is," agreed Asa. "Uncle Hirobei is annoyed with Kongomaru because he runs off sometimes and makes friends with undesirable people. He's awfully fond of food, and it's easy to tempt him away by giving him treats. I'm trying to cure him of the habit, but it takes time."

"Hirobei really takes a lot on himself, doesn't he?" remarked Matsuzo. "He acts as if he is master here."

"He would like to be," said Asa, her face expressionless. "He wants to marry my mother."

5

Before Matsuzo could talk further with Asa, Toshi returned and invited him to take refreshments in the main guest room of the house. It was a pleasant room, looking out onto a small but elegantly landscaped garden. Since it was winter, there was little to see, but here and there the scarlet petals of some winter camellias peeped above the snow to give splashes of color.

After Toshi left, a servant girl came to pour Matsuzo sake and placed before him a tray with dainty dishes of food to accompany the wine. Sipping the sake, Matsuzo looked around the room. The floor was covered with thick tatami mats, so much pleasanter than bare wooden floors on this cold day. There was a striking arrangement of waxy yellow plum blossoms in the alcove—Asa's work, Matsuzo suspected. By his elbow was a deep ceramic charcoal brazier, glazed in a shade of blue streaked with gray. Altogether it was a tastefully furnished room, with none of the showy display he had expected to see in the home of a prosperous merchant.

When the serving girl asked Matsuzo if he was ready for more substantial food, he nodded, remembering Zenta's advice to eat heartily whenever good food was offered. In their uncertain life they never knew when they would eat next. Matsuzo was just finishing the *zoni*, New Year's rice cakes cooked in broth, when Asa entered and asked if he had everything he needed.

"Yes, I'm full," said Matsuzo, putting down his chopsticks and replacing the lid on his soup bowl. "That was excellent zoni."

Asa smiled shyly. She waited until the serving girl had taken out the food tray and closed the door behind her. Then she said, "Are you and your friend staying at Uncle Ikken's house?"

Noticing a slight stiffness in the girl's manner, Matsuzo suspected that she had been ordered to question him and was embarrassed by the task. Since he had a number of questions himself, he welcomed the opportunity to exchange information. He explained Zenta's relation to the tea master and mentioned his surprise at the sad state of Ikken's house.

Asa flushed, as if sensing criticism. "We tried our best to help. My grandfather, my mother's father, admires Uncle Ikken tremendously. Grandfather spent some time as a merchant in Sakai and learned to appreciate the tea ceremony there. He is very proud of his family connection with such a famous tea master. After Shunken died, Grandfather even offered to let me live with Uncle Ikken and serve him as a daughter. You see, I was betrothed to Shunken."

Matsuzo was surprised. The girl looked very young, not much more than sixteen. However, she had sensitivity and a serenity not unlike Ikken's. He personally preferred girls who were more lively, but he admitted that one could grow to appreciate Asa's quiet kind of beauty. "You are very close to your uncle, aren't you?" he asked gently.

She nodded. "Ever since I was a child it has been assumed that Shunken and I would marry. Therefore Uncle Ikken took some pains to educate me to be a proper wife for a samurai. He even taught me the tea ceremony."

"It must have been a terrible blow for you when Shunken was killed," said Matsuzo.

"I admired him very much," said the girl quietly. "Of course I was also in awe of him, because he was more than ten years older than I was. Uncle Ikken was completely broken by Shunken's death. For the last three years he has shut himself in his house and refused to see people. He even dismissed all his servants."

"So that was it," said Matsuzo. "I thought they all had deserted him."

"We wanted to have him come and stay with us, at least for the New Year season," said Asa. "That was why we were visiting him last night, just before you arrived. But he refused to come."

The old tea master, heartbroken by the death of his son, would not want to stay at the home of his sour sister-in-law, especially when her meddling business manager was there, thought Matsuzo. "Ikken must spend all his time brooding, then," he said.

"I'm surprised to hear that Uncle Ikken has opened the door to you and your friend," said Asa. "He is actually letting you stay at his house?"

"Ikken had been like a father to Zenta," explained Matsuzo. "Perhaps when Zenta returned last night, it was almost like having his son come back."

"I hope this means that Uncle Ikken has broken his isolation at last," said Asa.

"I think Ikken had more preying on his mind than the death of his son," Matsuzo said. "There is something evil threatening this region, isn't there? A monster the villagers call the Vampire Cat?"

Asa shrank back and turned pale. Before she could speak, however, the door slid open and Hirobei's round, cheerful face appeared. "Are you making sure that our guest has everything he needs, Asa?" he asked and entered the room carrying a tray. "Here is a novel treat our young friend might enjoy."

He put down the tray, which contained a flat wooden box and a strange-looking slender bamboo tube. One end of the tube had a tiny metal bowl, not even large enough to hold a sparrow's egg.

Matsuzo watched curiously as Hirobei took some dark brown shreds from the box and rolled them into a small ball. He stuffed the ball into the tiny metal bowl and lit it with a taper. To Matsuzo's amazement Hirobei took a few puffs from the other end of the tube and released a cloud of acrid smoke. Asa coughed.

Hirobei tapped the tube against the charcoal brazier to dislodge the ashes. Making another little ball with the brown shreds and refilling the tiny bowl, he offered the tube to Matsuzo, saying, "This is tobacco, a plant brought by the Southern Barbarians. I've traveled a great deal and have actually met a few of the foreigners. Some people call them Long-Nosed Devils."

"I've already met some of these foreigners," said Matsuzo coldly. "They call themselves Portuguese."

"You've met the Southern Barbarians already?" said Hirobei, clearly surprised.

"Yes," said Matsuzo curtly. "You're not the only one who has traveled."

The merchant didn't seem offended by Matsuzo's curtness. For the first time he looked at the young ronin with genuine respect. "What did you think of the foreigners?"

Normally Matsuzo would have a great deal to say about the Portuguese, but now he was more interested in the subject of the monster cat. He said, "I was impressed by their firearms. And now if you don't mind—"

"Ah, yes, their firearms," said Hirobei, with a return of his ironical manner. "Naturally you warriors would care only about weapons. Now, we merchants are interested in all kinds of lesser things brought by the foreigners, such as tobacco. Do try some."

Matsuzo wrinkled his nose. "No, thank you. It smells terrible."

"People always think so at first," said Hirobei. "Once you get used to it, you'll enjoy it very much."

Matsuzo was increasingly annoyed by the merchant's

self-important air. "Nothing would persuade me to try this tobacco, as you call it. In fact I doubt that many people would take up this habit. It's just a passing fad." He waited impatiently for the merchant to leave so that he could resume questioning Asa.

But Hirobei said, "I couldn't help overhearing you when I was at the door just now. You were talking about the Vampire Cat that haunts the village?"

Perhaps Hirobei might be easier to question than Asa, who seemed petrified by the subject of the monster. "First of all, why do you call it the Vampire Cat?" Matsuzo asked the merchant.

"In the past three years four of the village girls have been found dead with their throats slashed," said Hirobei. "There is talk that this village is under a curse. A number of girls have told of being followed by something that mews like a cat, and the families of the dead girls reported that the victims suffered periods of dizziness and faintness before they were attacked. They believed a ghost cat was draining their vitality before finally killing them."

Asa made a small choking sound. Hirobei turned to her and said, "You can stop worrying now, Asa. This young gentleman and his friend have come to protect us from the Cat."

Matsuzo looked suspiciously at the merchant. Was he being sarcastic? "Well, I believe that the so-called Vampire Cat is a human being," the young ronin said stiffly. Kongomaru's attack on the piece of black cloth had convinced him. Hirobei might be scornful of the dog's intelligence, but Matsuzo was sure Kongomaru had recognized the scrap as coming from the clothing of the murderer.

"If a human being is behind these murders, he must be insane," said Hirobei. In his round face, his eyes were thoughtful. "I've heard that your friend is a noted warrior. He might be able to find the murderer and destroy him."

The tavern keeper had kept busy spreading the word about Zenta, thought Matsuzo. "We suspect that the band of medicine peddlers here might be accomplices of the Cat," he said.

Hirobei did not seem surprised at the suggestion. "Then the idea has occurred to you as well? I wondered about the excellent profits made by the peddlers from the sale of their medicine."

"Of course the idea has occurred to us!" said Matsuzo. "Give us credit for some intelligence!" The merchant's condescending attitude annoyed him. Nevertheless he admitted that the man was shrewd, with the cunning of his kind. Perhaps he could contribute some useful ideas. "How many men are there in the peddler band?" he asked Hirobei.

The merchant did some mental calculation. "Let me see. There is Ryutaro, the leader, a very tough fighter by the way. Most of the men look like ronin. Before they took up the quack medicine business, they must have seen action as bandits. Then there are various other men, vagabonds, rogues, what have you, who must have been displaced by the wars. I would say not less than thirty men, but not many more either."

"A sizable group," said Matsuzo thoughtfully. "But if these men are just rogues and vagabonds, we should be able to put some fear into them."

"Don't underestimate them," warned Hirobei. "They are well drilled and organized. Ryutaro is a resourceful leader and knows how to maintain discipline. He has set up his headquarters in a deserted temple not far from here. In addition to the money they get from selling medicine, they practice some banditry on the side and help themselves to the harvests of farmers in the region."

"Zenta will find a way to defeat these men. He has dealt with bandits before."

"Then there is the threat of the Cat," said Hirobei. "The people here do believe in the ghost cat, you know."

"They won't for long," said Matsuzo. "We'll soon show them that the so-called Vampire Cat is just a man dressed up in skins and making mewing noises."

"Oh, no, you're wrong about the Cat!" cried Asa. "No human being could do the things the Cat does!"

Matsuzo stared at the girl in surprise. She seemed convinced of the supernatural powers of the Cat.

Asa swallowed and continued, "The family of one of the victims even called in an exorcist. He prayed and tried to seal her room against evil spirits, but the girl still suffered from fainting spells and couldn't escape being killed."

"How did the girl die?" asked Matsuzo.

"They all had their throats cut," whispered Asa. "The first girl was also badly scratched. When other village girls said they heard strange mewing noises, some of the women remembered the dying curse of a warrior killed in a battle near here, and people began to talk about the Vampire Cat who drank blood."

In spite of himself, Matsuzo was chilled by the story. "Did the girls die at home, or were they attacked in some lonely spot?" he asked.

Hirobei answered. "The first two victims were found in the open, one near a rice paddy and one on a footpath in the hills. After that, parents began to warn their daughters about the dangers of venturing out alone."

"And the other two victims?" asked Matsuzo.

"In the third case the girl was found dead in her room, in spite of the efforts of the exorcist. The parents of the fourth girl also called in the exorcist, but it didn't help. In this case the girl was not the only one overcome by faintness. Her parents and younger brother, who were sleeping in the same room, were also unconscious. But the girl was the only one killed. Her body was found in the garden."

"How do you know so much about this, Uncle Hirobei?" asked Asa, looking surprised. "I thought you were away on business during those occasions."

"Naturally I found out all the facts I could after I came back," said Hirobei calmly.

Matsuzo thought about the last two deaths. "Faintness and unconsciousness could be caused by poison."

Hirobei smiled. "Other people have thought of that, too, including the parents of the fourth girl. When she started to complain of faintness, they immediately took great precautions over the food. But she was killed in spite of all their watch and care."

"What about the exorcist?" asked Matsuzo suddenly.

"Did the same man perform the rites for both girls? Who was he, anyway? A Buddhist priest?"

"Ah, you're wondering about the exorcist, too," said the merchant. "I made some inquiries about him as soon as I heard about the affair."

"Well? What did you learn about the exorcist?"

"It seems that he is a local boy who trained to be a priest," answered Hirobei. "Not being particularly bright, he didn't advance very far, but he did learn enough priestly mumbo-jumbo to fool the country people here. He is a thin, weakly fellow, and you're mistaken if you think that he is the Vampire Cat."

Hirobei certainly had quick answers to all the questions. Matsuzo began to see that the problem of the Cat was not so simple as he had thought. It was small wonder that the villagers were so terrified. "When did the peddlers arrive and begin to sell their medicine?" he asked.

Again Hirobei wore that condescending smile. "I knew you were going to ask that. The peddlers came after the second murder and immediately sold large quantities of their medicine to most of the families here with daughters. Even some of the old hags bought medicine for themselves."

"Yes, I know," said Matsuzo. "The tavern keeper's wife bought some."

"Not everyone believed in the medicine," said Hirobei. "The family of the fourth girl preferred to call in the exorcist rather than buy the medicine."

"Did the medicine work?" asked Matsuzo. He quickly corrected himself. "I mean, were there any attacks on girls who were taking the medicine?"

Hirobei hesitated before answering. "There hasn't been another murder, certainly. But I'm not sure whether the girls are really safe." He glanced at Asa. "You had a narrow escape last year, didn't you?"

Asa shivered. "I'm sure that without Kongomaru I would have been murdered."

Matsuzo was horrified. "What happened?"

The girl seemed reluctant even to speak of her experience. "Go on. Tell him," urged Hirobei.

"The village girls were saying that something was following them around." Asa's voice was shaky. "When Uncle Ikken heard, he insisted on getting Kongomaru for us."

"He would have done better to find a smaller dog who eats less and does more," muttered Hirobei.

"That's not fair!" cried Asa. "A smaller dog wouldn't have saved me." She swallowed. "One dark night when I was walking along the path near Uncle Ikken's house, I heard something rustling behind me, and then I heard a hideous mewing noise."

It was exactly like their own experience, thought Matsuzo. Asa had not been imagining things.

"Kongomaru started to bark furiously," continued Asa. "He suddenly dashed into the bushes and got into a terrible fight with a large animal. It was no match for Kongomaru, and after a fierce struggle, it had to run off. Kongomaru was scratched and bleeding, and one of his ears was badly torn. But he saved my life."

Matsuzo agreed. Any warlord would be fortunate to have a retainer as brave and loyal as this dog. He had one more question, however, but he didn't want to ask it in front of the frightened girl. He looked out the door leading to the garden and said, "Speaking of Kongomaru, I thought he was sitting on the veranda. Where is he?"

Asa got up and looked into the garden. "I'm afraid he's gone again," she sighed. "I'll have to go look for him."

"That stupid dog!" said Hirobei. "He's so greedy that he makes friends with any stranger who offers him food. You'd better get rid of him and find a more reliable protector, Asa."

Asa looked like an embarrassed mother whose child accepted candy from strangers. "Kongomaru will be back. He has always returned before, Uncle Hirobei."

When the door closed behind the girl, Hirobei said, "Asa dotes on that dog. But one of these days, he will be gone just when she needs him most."

"Kongomaru is absolutely loyal!" protested Matsuzo.

Hirobei looked skeptical. "You have something else to ask me, haven't you?" he asked.

The young ronin nodded. "Can you tell me whether any of the victims were raped?"

The merchant was not smiling now. His expression was somber as he answered, "Since the victims were all girls who were young and pretty, that was the first thought that occurred to us. The answer is that they were not attacked sexually, although the first two girls were badly scratched and their clothes were torn. If the murderer was a man, it wasn't desire for the girls that drove him to it."

Then he added, "Because of this, the villagers believe

more than ever that it wasn't a man, but a monstrous cat."

On the other side of the papered door Asa moved away quietly, for she had heard enough. She knew that the two men wanted her out of the room before they discussed the question of whether the Cat raped his victims, a topic they thought too shocking for her ears. They didn't know that she had already heard the maidservants and the village girls discuss the subject in some detail.

Asa was sorry that she had shown her fear to the young samurai just now. He must have thought her a poor-spirited thing, trembling at the first sign of danger. After Shunken's death her uncle had wanted to arrange another marriage for her. He might even be considering these two samurai staying at his house! At this thought she felt herself blushing.

They were both good-looking in their different ways. The taller one she had seen only briefly the night before. He seemed cool and self-assured, and she felt some awe toward him. It was similar to the feeling she had had for Shunken. But since wives were supposed to stand in awe of their husbands, that feeling was altogether appropriate.

The younger one, Matsuzo, seemed much more approachable, and she already liked him. But from the way he looked over the maids she suspected that he had a roving eye. A girl married to him might have frequent cause for jealousy, something she knew a proper wife should never feel.

Uncle Ikken had taught her the proper behavior for the wife of a samurai. He had taken more trouble with her education than most fathers did with their daughters. She loved her uncle and wanted to please him. She resolved to show her uncle—and the two young samurai—that she could be brave and enterprising.

6

Earlier that day, after Matsuzo had left, Zenta had gone to Ikken's study to pay his respects. Although the tea master had greeted him warmly, his manner had been distracted and he had started at the slightest noise. Years ago Zenta had learned how to achieve composure from Ikken, and now he found it extremely painful to see his teacher's agitation.

As he left Ikken's house for the village, he was resolved more than ever to end quickly the reign of terror that was crushing everyone here. His first objective was to question the tavern keeper.

Walking down the street toward the tavern, Zenta saw the village more clearly now that there was no falling snow to blur the visibility. This morning there were attempts at New Year's decorations on both sides of the street. The green pine boughs, the plaited ritual straw and folded paper, looked brave against the wretched houses.

These decorations represented hope, since New Year's was considered the official beginning of spring. The region was in the Snow Country, and there would still be several months of heavy snow before any real break in the weather would come. Nevertheless the New Year's festival served to remind people that there was an end to the long winter.

There was hope, too, in the open shutters of the houses on either side of the street. Zenta could feel the eyes of the villagers on him, but this morning they seemed less frightened of showing their faces. He couldn't tell from their expressions whether the people regarded him as a possible defender against the rapacious medicine peddlers or as one more oppressor. In a country that had been torn by civil wars for almost a hundred years, the people had learned to treat any armed man with caution.

The village tavern, being the most prosperous place on the street, was decorated more elaborately than the rest of the houses. In addition to the pine boughs, there were branches of bamboo and fern. Zenta smiled to see that the thrifty tavern keeper had living pine trees in tubs, so that he could use them year after year instead of cutting fresh ones each time.

By some means the news of Zenta's approach had already reached the tavern, and the tavern keeper was at the door with a beaming face. "Please honor my house again with your presence!" he cried. "We will try to make up for our poor fare last night."

Entering, Zenta saw that seasonal decoration had been put up inside the house as well. Tangerines and rice cakes were arranged on a table, together with a "Treasure Ship" made of plaited straw and depicting the Seven Lucky Gods. Zenta eyed the pile of rice cakes with misgivings. Had they been salvaged from the scrimmage last night? He remembered the tavern keeper's thrift and thought he detected a grayish hue to the cakes.

After the tavern keeper saw his guest seated, he hesitated. Some faint memory may have stirred in his mind. "Have I had the good fortune to meet you before yesterday, sir?"

Zenta smiled politely. "If you have, the good fortune was all yours."

The tavern keeper puzzled over the remark for a moment, then appeared to give it up. He turned and yelled at his wife to bring food and drink. The woman who presently came out carrying a tray of drinks was the same one Zenta had seen briefly in the back of the house helping to make rice cakes. He didn't remember her from his first visit to the village ten years ago. She was many years younger than her husband, and she had small features in a round white face which reminded Zenta of the folk mask *Otafuku*, Good Fortune. Many people would consider her plumpness, white skin, and red cheeks attractive, but she was not a type that appealed to him.

"Hurry up with the drinks!" snarled her husband. "Can't you see our guest is waiting? You're getting fat and slow, you lazy slattern. You eat too much."

Looking at the tavern keeper's mean, wizened face, Zenta thought that he would be unlikely to permit over-eating in the house. But the woman's tiny eyes shone with a cunning greed. She would think of a way to get food if anyone could.

Zenta tasted the wine and found it much better than what he had received the night before. He suspected that the tavern keeper wanted something from him.

He was not mistaken. Pulling up a cushion made of straw, the tavern keeper sat down and began in a voice oozing with flattery, "I've been telling all my neighbors about the way you routed those peddlers, sir."

Zenta tried a piece of dried squid and chewed it thoughtfully. "I'm not sure that the peddlers were routed permanently. Didn't the leader say something about bringing reinforcements?"

The tavern keeper's eyes flickered with alarm, but he recovered quickly. "If you and your friend can kill the leader, Ryutaro, and one or two of his chief henchmen, the rest of the band will simply dissolve. Most of them are just scoundrels looking for excitement. I'm sure you can show them more than they bargained for."

"And what about the monster cat?" asked Zenta. "Will it dissolve, too, when Ryutaro is gone?"

The tavern keeper gave a scornful sniff. "I've never believed in the monster. You see, I happen to know that my wife invented the story of the Vampire Cat."

"What!" Zenta turned and stared at the tavern keeper's wife.

"But it's turning out to be true!" said the woman.

67

"There really is a Vampire Cat killing the girls in this village." Suddenly she stared at Zenta's throat and screamed.

"What's the matter?" demanded her husband.

"That scratch! How did you get it?"

Ikken had shown a similar fear on seeing the scratch, thought Zenta. "It happened last night when I was going up the hill," he said. "I had a brief struggle with some animal, and in the confusion I received this scratch."

"You were struggling with the Vampire Cat!" cried the woman. "It tears out the throats of its victims and drinks their blood!"

There was no doubt that her fear was genuine. It was also contagious, and Zenta's hand involuntarily went to his throat. That snarling, vicious thing last night had intended to kill, he was sure of that.

"Tell me more about the murders," Zenta said to the woman. "How many girls have been killed?"

"Four, altogether. They all had their throats slashed, and some had scratches on their faces—deep, ugly scratches." The woman's plump, white face quivered and she moaned. "It must have been the work of the ghost cat."

"Nonsense!" said the tavern keeper. "I still say the murderer is a man. He was angry because the girls wouldn't look at him, and he got his revenge by attacking them."

He turned to his wife and said, "He won't bother with an ugly thing like you, so stop wasting my money on useless medicines!"

"You said the Cat only attacked young girls," said his

wife. "But last night it attacked this gentleman. Nobody is safe!"

"I think it attacked me because I was trying to surprise it by coming from behind," said Zenta. "And it's not certain that I got this scratch from the beast. It could have been from a tree branch." He still thought that he had been too far away to grapple with the animal. Another possibility, a frightening one, was that the thing had monstrously long arms.

"But I've also been cursed," moaned the tavern keeper's wife. "The whole village has been cursed by that dying warrior!"

"What dying warrior?" demanded Zenta.

The tavern keeper looked uncomfortable. "There was a battle here three years ago. After the battle a lot of corpses were lying about, and the women of the village, including my wife here, decided to help themselves to some of the dead men's weapons and armor, things they could sell."

Zenta looked at the woman with shocked loathing. As a samurai, he was fully prepared for a violent death, by his own hand or honorably in battle. But he was revolted by the thought that scavengers like this woman might come after the battle to plunder his dead body.

"Dead men don't need weapons or armor, do they?" said the woman defensively. "And we common people always suffer the most from the wars. It's only right that we should help ourselves to what we can. A good suit of armor can fetch enough money to feed a family for months."

Zenta swallowed his disgust. He needed information.

"You were talking about a *dying* warrior. That means you were looting someone who was still alive?"

"He looked quite dead," mumbled the woman. "I was just about to take his helmet when he opened his eyes and cursed me."

"Well, you didn't take the curse seriously at first," said her husband. "When the first girl was killed, you started telling the story of the curse so that our customers would stay around longer and drink more. *You're* the one who thought of the Vampire Cat, because of the scratches and the mewing. You told me so yourself."

"Yes, but I really believe in the Cat now! I've seen its supernatural powers!"

"What supernatural powers?" asked Zenta.

"The Cat can drain the life and vitality from a girl and leave her unconscious," said the woman. She turned to her husband and said, "You can't explain how it was done, either."

"Some drug, perhaps?" suggested Zenta. "The medicine peddlers might have a number of things that could cause unconsciousness."

"No, it wasn't that," admitted the tavern keeper. "The parents of the girls had thought of that already and kept a careful watch on the food. On the advice of an exorcist they even sealed all the cracks in the windows and doors with strips of paper to prevent evil spirits from entering at night."

"Wasn't that unwise?" said Zenta. "When a charcoal brazier is burning in a tightly closed room, the air can become foul and poisonous. That alone would make people faint."

"They've thought of that, too," said the tavern keeper gloomily. "The parents of the dead girls insisted that the air had not been foul-smelling."

Zenta was baffled. "It's hard to see how a murderer could have entered and killed the girl if her windows and doors were all sealed with paper."

"The girls were not killed while their rooms were sealed," said the tavern keeper. "In both cases they had fainting spells, but they were killed later. The first two girls weren't even home. They were attacked in the open."

"That's quite different, then," said Zenta slowly. The problem was beginning to look less impossible. "The person who committed the murder and the person who caused the fainting spells could even be two distinct people."

The tavern keeper nodded eagerly. "What I believe is that some madman is killing these girls, and the medicine peddlers saw the opportunity to make money. So they thought of a way to cause dizziness and fainting spells and frightened people into spending money for their medicine."

He turned and looked disgustedly at his wife. "And you helped them with your story of the dying man's curse!"

Zenta thought over the tavern keeper's words and felt inclined to agree in part. The man was very acute, especially when it was a matter involving money. But Zenta remembered the fear in Ikken's eyes. The tea master was one of the wisest men he knew, and if he was frightened, the problem was more formidable than the tavern keeper had claimed. Suddenly Zenta was roused from his thoughts by the sound of screams down the street.

"Go and see what's happening," the tavern keeper ordered his wife.

In a few moments the woman returned panting, her little eyes shining with fear and excitement. "The Cat has killed another girl! It's the daughter of Jiro the carpenter!"

Zenta jumped up and thrust his long sword back into his sash. "We'd better go to Jiro's house and see what has happened."

The carpenter's house consisted of only a front room, used as a workshop, and a back room, used by the family as their living quarters. Like the rest of the houses in the village, it showed the owner's hard struggle to stay ahead of starvation. On the front gate was an attempt at New Year's decoration, a pathetic touch of festivity.

There was a crowd at the gate and in the front room, but it parted quickly to let Zenta and the tavern keeper through. A few of the people looked at the ronin with something like hope, but the eyes of most of them contained only dull despair.

In the family room the victim's body had been arranged and covered with a quilt. Over the face was a white cloth. On either side of the body sat the parents. The father's face was gray and vacant with shock, and the mother's face was blotched with weeping. A pretty girl of about twelve sat behind the mother, probably a younger sister of the dead girl. She looked too dazed to feel any real grief.

Zenta bowed his respects to the dead and lifted a

corner of the white cloth to look at the girl's face. Although prepared for the sight, he was still shocked by the deep gashes across the neck. Too jagged to be made by a sword or a knife, they really looked as if they had been made by the claws of a beast.

"Was she killed in this room?" asked Zenta.

The father didn't even seem to hear the question. It was the mother, still hoarse from weeping, who answered. "No, I found her lying outside the kitchen door. I thought she had fainted, and when I turned her over, I saw . . . I saw . . . " She stopped, overcome by sobs.

"I'm going to examine the kitchen," said Zenta. Since the body had been moved, any useful clue would probably be destroyed. Still, he might find something.

As he rose to leave, he was arrested by the father's voice. "She was killed by the Vampire Cat. No human being could have done it."

"Nonsense!" said the tavern keeper. "Why do you people keep insisting on the supernatural?"

"Only the Vampire Cat could have done it," repeated the father dully. "There were no footprints in the snow."

"You must be blind!" said the tavern keeper angrily. "I saw hundreds of footprints!"

The mother looked up. "Jiro is right. When we first found our daughter, she was lying outside the door of the kitchen facing the back garden. The snow out there was completely untouched."

Zenta quickly left the room and went into the kitchen. The blood still showed at the back entrance. In the back garden there were many footprints, presumably made by the neighbors when they came. The garden was very small, the size one would expect for the carpenter's meager home, but it was still difficult to see how the murderer could have reached the girl without stepping across the snow—unless he was a member of the household. Looking at the grieving parents and the younger sister, Zenta knew that that was impossible.

Then there was his own experience. Zenta was now forced to face the uncomfortable fact that the scratch on his neck might not have been made by a tree branch after all. Into his mind came a vision of a monster with arms three times as long as those of a human being.

Zenta resolutely pushed the thought aside. There had to be a logical explanation, and he would find it.

When he returned to the inside of the house, he found the tavern keeper talking excitedly to a circle of attentive listeners. Seeing Zenta the tavern keeper said, "I've just heard from Jiro that his daughter was taking the medicine bought from the peddlers. And she was still murdered! That proves that those men are quacks and their medicine utterly useless. Those scoundrels have been cheating us all along!"

There was an angry murmur from the others in the room. One man said, "For two years our family hasn't eaten one grain of rice, only millet. We saved everything we could in order to buy the medicine!"

"We wanted to get a new kimono for our daughter," sobbed the mother of the dead girl. "The old one was outgrown and all the seams were let out. But we decided to use the money for the medicine. We thought at least she would be alive!"

"You will drive out those cheating peddlers, won't you?" the tavern keeper asked Zenta.

"You'd better tell me first how many men there are in the band," said Zenta.

"Ryutaro, the leader, is the most dangerous one," said the tavern keeper. "Try to take care of him first."

Zenta detected evasiveness. "Very well, I'll try to take care of Ryutaro. It would be helpful if he agrees to meet me alone. Now tell me about his reinforcements."

"There are at least thirty men in the band, and they have a strong hideout not far from the village!" said one of the other men.

The tavern keeper turned angrily on the speaker. "Most of those men are just cowards, like you, so they don't count for much!"

"I'll probably need help—" began Zenta. Before he could go on, there was a general movement in the room.

"I've left my daughter at home, and I'd better hurry back to make sure that she is safe," murmured one man, getting up and bowing to Jiro and his wife.

Others quickly followed suit. In a few minutes the only people left with the bereaved parents were Zenta and the tavern keeper. The latter looked disgustedly at the retreating backs. "Cowards!"

"It doesn't look as if we'll have superiority of numbers," said Zenta dryly. "To attack the peddlers, we'd better think of some strategy, then. Unless you think we can immobilize them first with rice paste?"

"I'll help you," declared the tavern keeper. "My wife can do something, too, even if I have to kick her into it."

75

He was obviously determined to fight the peddlers with Zenta's help. For three years they had been draining the village of all the money that would normally have gone into his coffers.

After taking leave of the carpenter and his wife, Zenta discussed plans with the tavern keeper as they walked back to the tavern. "One thing is in our favor," said Zenta. "I thought at first that the murderer might have instructions from Ryutaro to refrain from killing girls who have taken the medicine. But this latest murder shows that the Cat is not under Ryutaro's control. He might even clash with the peddlers eventually. In that case—"

He broke off, his eyes caught by a most unexpected sight. At the end of the street, walking briskly away from them, was Ryutaro, the leader of the peddlers. Trotting by his side was a big white dog with black ears and a tan patch on his back. He looked for all the world like Kongomaru.

7

"I have to see what this is all about," said Zenta, starting after the peddler and the dog.

"What?" cried the tavern keeper, running after him. "You don't mean to follow them in broad daylight? I thought we were going to get your friend and plan a surprise attack on their hideout."

"If the peddlers' hideout is really well defended," said Zenta, "a surprise attack would be impossible, anyway. With or without the help of my friend, we have no hope of making a successful assault. I'm just trying to find out why that peddler is so friendly with the dog."

"The peddlers won't be very happy to see us, not after what happened at my tavern last night," muttered the tavern keeper.

Seeing that the man was really frightened, Zenta said, "You don't have to come with me. I want you to find my friend and tell him where I'm going. He is visiting the widowed sister-in-law of the tea master. Do you know where she lives?"

"He is visiting Toshi? Everyone knows where she lives. She owns that big house on the other side of the rice paddies."

After the tavern keeper had left on his errand, Zenta hurried in the direction taken by the peddler. The man and the dog had entered a bamboo grove and were no longer in sight, but Zenta had no difficulty following the dog's prints in the snow. He knew that he was taking a risk, but at the tavern last night the expression of the leader Ryutaro had not been completely hostile.

Still, it was possible that he might have to fight with members of the peddler band. As Zenta's skill with the sword grew, he felt a need—a compulsion, even—to pit himself against growing odds. It was the only way to improve. Someday he might find the odds too great, but that was preferable to stagnation.

After another turn in the road, Zenta caught sight of the man and the dog again. He was sure that the man was Ryutaro, the leader of the band. The dog would run ahead of his companion and then come bounding back, giving short, happy barks. Every frisky movement showed his keen enjoyment of the sun, the snow, the whole outing.

If the dog were really Kongomaru, he was neglecting his guard duties, thought Zenta. Asa might not be as safe as she thought.

The dog stopped and stood sniffing the air. Ryutaro pulled out a tidbit and tossed it to the dog, who bolted it down greedily, and the two went on. If the peddler was aware that Zenta was behind him, he gave no sign.

The bamboo gave way to pine trees, which soon grew so thick that Zenta again lost sight of Ryutaro and the dog. He became more and more certain that the peddler knew he was being followed. Perhaps at the moment he was preparing an ambush. Zenta pressed his left thumb against the guard of his sword, loosening the sword in the scabbard so that he could draw instantly. He had no wish to start hostilities, but he wanted to be prepared.

All at once Zenta found himself in a clearing, and in the middle of it he saw a small Buddhist temple. The deeply pitched roof was covered with snow, giving the building an impression of neatness and cleanliness. But there were signs that a long time had passed since monks had cared for the place. The steps leading up to the front veranda sagged, and the railing around the veranda was broken in several places. The snow on the ground around the building was churned, showing the signs of many feet. But no one was in sight and the silence was complete.

Zenta heard a faint rustle behind him. He whirled around with his hand on the hilt of his sword. When he saw it was the big white dog, he relaxed. He had already made Kongomaru's acquaintance, and the dog, after sniffing his hand last night, had accepted him as a friend.

But the dog seemed to have forgotten the meeting, for he was anything but friendly. His hair stiffened and his eyes glittered strangely. A low growl buzzed deep in his throat.

For a moment Zenta thought that this dog was not Kongomaru at all. Then he saw the torn black ear. Without doubt it was Asa's dog. Knowing that the best way to approach a suspicious dog was to show no fear, Zenta held out his hand and said in a quiet, friendly voice, "Kongomaru, what are you doing here without your mistress?"

It was the wrong tactic. Before Zenta could pull his hand back the dog sprang. A numbing pain shot up his arm as the dog clamped his powerful jaws around his right wrist. In pure instinct Zenta's left hand reached for his sword. But he didn't draw, for he remembered that this was Kongomaru, Asa's protector.

"Don't touch your sword," said a voice.

Zenta turned his head and saw Ryutaro and his men standing behind him. The leader of the peddlers continued, "I'll call off the dog if you surrender your swords. He can cripple your hand permanently before you can kill him."

Kongomaru tightened his jaws. Zenta took a deep breath. With a great effort he kept his voice steady as he said, "It's better to lose my hand than my life."

Seconds passed, and they seemed like hours. Finally Ryutaro said, "Very well, keep your swords. Down, Kongomaru!"

The dog's jaws loosed slightly, but he still growled and hung on, apparently unable to conquer his distrust of Zenta.

"Down, I say! Drop his hand, Kongomaru!"

After repeated orders from the peddler, the dog finally

relaxed his grip. "Put a halter around that dog's neck and keep him out of the way," Ryutaro ordered his men.

At the return of circulation Zenta's wrist throbbed with pain. He looked at his hand and was relieved to see that it was not lacerated, only badly bruised and beginning to swell.

"Put some snow on it. It will reduce the swelling," Ryutaro advised.

Zenta scooped up some snow with his left hand and followed Ryutaro's suggestion. After a while the sharp agony subsided to a dull ache.

Ryutaro looked on with a worried frown. "I don't want to see your hand crippled. On the contrary . . ."

Kongomaru, now safely tethered to a tree, showed his teeth in a snarl. Ryutaro looked from the dog to Zenta. "Kongomaru has taken a dislike to you for some reason."

"I don't understand that dog at all!" said Zenta. "Yesterday we became friends, and now he behaves as if I'm his worst enemy. Nothing about him surprises me any more. You don't suppose that the Vampire Cat is really Kongomaru in disguise?"

At the mention of the Cat there was a rustle from Ryutaro's men, and Zenta saw that some of them shuffled uncomfortably. Their leader's face was unreadable. Ignoring his men he said to Zenta, "Let's go inside and warm ourselves. I have a proposition to make."

Startled, Zenta rose and followed Ryutaro to the temple building. As he went up the sagging steps, he flexed his hand experimentally. It would be some time before the hand would be useful again.

The inside of the building no longer bore any resemblance to a temple. The large hall with its two rows of pillars was now cluttered with arms, packs, bedding, and even cooking utensils. Ryutaro looked around at the disorder and grunted in disgust. "What a rabble! I keep telling them that you can't get ready for action quickly if your pack is a mess."

He searched around until he found two flat straw cushions. Shaking off a cloud of dust and bits of straw, he offered one to Zenta.

The ronin sat down cross-legged on the cushions and rested his throbbing hand on his knee. "Is there any reason why a medicine peddler should be ready for action quickly?" he asked.

Ryutaro's thick brows met in an angry frown, but a moment later his face cleared and he laughed, again showing his sharp white teeth. "Of course we have to be ready! There are dangerous people who throw rice paste around, for example. Three of my men are still trying to work the stuff out of their hair."

Zenta decided that there was something almost likable about Ryutaro. The man had probably served as an officer, and in normal times he might have lived out his life as a loyal samurai in the service of some feudal lord. But in this period of civil wars many feudal lords had been overthrown and their followers had become ronin. Some of the luckier ones found employment with other warlords. Some gave up their profession of arms to become merchants, farmers, physicians, teachers, or anything they could put their hand to. The less scrupulous ones lived by preying on people weaker than themselves.

"Bring some sake," Ryutaro ordered one of his men. "Put some more charcoal in that brazier and bring it over. It's freezing in here."

When the man started to take charcoal out of a metal basket, Ryutaro yelled at him, "Not that charcoal, you idiot!"

At this, another man sitting in the corner chuckled and said, "That's my charcoal. I'm the only one who is supposed to touch it." He rose, seized the metal basket from the other man, and made off with it, still chuckling.

Zenta thought that the metal basket looked familiar. But at the moment he was more interested in the strange man who was carrying it off. The man had short hair, a sign that at some time or another his head had been cropped. He was probably a Buddhist priest, and this was borne out by his robes, although they were too tattered and dirty to indicate his sect. All his movements were untidy, as if his joints were too loose. His head, heavy for his neck, lolled around as he walked out of the room, giggling at a private joke.

"That's our exorcist," Ryutaro told Zenta. "Don't pay any attention to him. He is little better than an imbecile, but because of his strangeness, the villagers believe he has unusual powers. They call him in whenever they need to expel demons."

A few of the men laughed. Zenta thought it likely that, far from expelling demons, the exorcist helped to spread terror among the villagers. Ryutaro frowned with annoyance at his men. "You two!" he snapped at two of the laughing men. "You've been idling all day. Now get on your feet and find some clean bedding for our guest.

He can have the room that used to be the chief priest's study."

"Don't bother on my account," said Zenta. "I won't be staying."

The men laughed even more loudly. When the sake arrived Ryutaro said to his men, "Now shut up. I have something to discuss with our guest."

The men fell silent, and those who were at the far end of the room came closer, unwilling to miss what their leader was going to say.

Ryutaro's eyes were intent on Zenta. He said abruptly, "How would you like to be joint leader of this band with me?"

Covering his surprise Zenta made a pretense of fumbling left-handedly with his square wooden wine cup. He wanted time to think. Finally he raised his eyes to Ryutaro and said, "I don't think I want to go into the quack medicine business."

Ryutaro banged his wooden cup down on the floor angrily. "You know perfectly well that we're not really medicine peddlers!"

"I'm not sure that I like the business of extorting money from frightened villagers any better," murmured Zenta.

There was an angry rumble from some of the men in the room. Ryutaro stood up and roared, "Quiet! If you can't keep quiet, then get out and stay out!"

The men subsided, but some of them continued to shake their heads angrily. Ryutaro tossed down his cup of sake and poured some more for himself and Zenta.

"All right, it was a shabby trick to squeeze money from these villagers, but plenty of ronin have done worse things to make a living. Besides, these villagers deserve to pay. Did you know that there was a battle here three years ago, and afterward the people helped to hunt down the defeated so they could collect a reward?"

One of the men said, "The women of the village went back to the battlefield like ghouls and looted the dead bodies!"

"I don't approve of the villagers' behavior any more than you do," said Zenta. "But I've just come from seeing Jiro the carpenter, whose daughter has been brutally murdered. However badly the villagers behaved, you can't justify murder."

"But we didn't commit the murders—" began one of the men. He broke off at a look from his leader.

"The murders were committed by the Cat," said Ryutaro. "If you agree to my proposal, we'll combine forces to oppose him."

Some of his men stirred uneasily. One of them said, "Ryutaro, if the Cat hears about this, he'll kill you! You must be insane if you think you can get away with it."

Ryutaro turned fiercely on the speaker. "The Cat is the one who is insane! This morning he killed a girl when he knew perfectly well that we sold medicine to her family. He is getting so unbalanced that we won't be able to predict what he will do next."

"The Cat is too strong for us," said another man. "We'll have to continue doing what he tells us, Ryutaro."

Zenta saw that all the men were in deadly fear of the

85

Cat, even Ryutaro, who did not look like a timid man. "What makes the Cat so strong?" he asked. "Do you really believe in his supernatural powers?"

Ryutaro laughed grimly. "There is nothing supernatural about his powers. You might not believe me, but these villagers brought the Vampire Cat curse on themselves! After the first murder they were the ones who spread the story of the ghost cat who drank blood."

Having heard the confession of the tavern keeper's wife, Zenta knew that Ryutaro spoke the truth. The peddlers were not the ones who started the Vampire Cat story. "But you came and took advantage of the rumors to sell your so-called medicine?"

"We used powdered bamboo leaves mixed with fish gall," said Ryutaro with a grin. "Of course the villagers were convinced that anything that tasted so horrible had to be effective!"

"Tell me," said Zenta, "since you know that there is nothing supernatural about the Cat, why are you all so afraid of him?"

"He is mad," said Ryutaro shortly. "He has all the diabolical cunning of the insane, and I don't mind admitting that he frightens me."

"You want to break away from him because you won't be able to sell any more of your medicine, now that everyone knows it's useless?" asked Zenta.

"I'm sick of peddling medicine!" said Ryutaro. "It never brought in much money, anyway. What can you get from a few miserable peasants? I want to go away and start something different."

A few of his men nodded agreement. "These murders

are bad, and we don't want any more of them," one man said.

Most of the others still seemed frightened at the thought of defying the Cat, however, and several glanced back nervously over their shoulders.

Zenta now had the information he wanted. The Cat was a man of extraordinary cleverness and force, since he could control this band of outlaws and make them take his orders. Ryutaro's eagerness to enlist Zenta's aid suggested that the Cat was a formidable swordsman as well.

His next problem was to extricate himself from the peddlers' hideout. That might be more difficult than he had originally expected, because of the injury to his hand. He looked up to find Ryutaro staring earnestly at him. "Join our band," said the peddler. "I know your reputation, and I believe that with your help we can defeat the Cat."

"I'll gladly join your fight against the Cat," said Zenta. "But I'm not sure I want to be a leader in your band."

"You must promise to join the band," insisted Ryutaro. "We don't want to go back to our days of starvation and petty banditry. With you as a leader our band can become a force to reckon with in this region. But if you refuse to join, we'll have to continue working for the Cat. At least his plan can bring in money."

Zenta remembered the loss of Ikken's tea utensils and felt himself growing angry. "You mean the money you get from terrorizing villagers and lonely old men?"

"The Cat is working on a plan to get hold of the money that the girl Asa will inherit from her grandfather," said one of the men. "It's a huge fortune."

Up to then Zenta had thought of the Cat as a madman who was driven by a compulsion to attack young girls. Now it seemed that the actions of the Cat had a more specific purpose. "What is the Cat's plan?" he demanded.

"I can't tell you that unless you accept my offer," said Ryutaro.

Zenta knew he had to escape, and quickly. He needed to find out the details about the Cat's plans concerning Asa. Nursing his wrist, now puffy and discolored, he said, "I'll have to think it over."

Ryutaro looked regretful. "That means you refuse. Too bad. One of the men here is certain to report our talk to the Cat, so I'll have to prove my loyalty to him by killing you first."

But Zenta had already seen the intention on Ryutaro's face. As the peddler finished speaking and whipped out his sword, Zenta acted even more quickly. In one bound he was on his feet, with a pillar protecting his back and his sword in his left hand.

"You'd better give up," advised Ryutaro. "With only one good hand, do you think you'd have a chance against us?"

"Why don't you try to find out?" asked Zenta.

Before anyone could make the next move, they heard a furious barking. "Kongomaru!" muttered Ryutaro. "What's the matter with him?"

In the instant while the attention of the others was distracted, Zenta seized his chance. He kicked hard at the nearest charcoal brazier, knocking it over and scattering the hot ashes. Paying no attention to the cries of pain as the smouldering charcoal landed, Zenta rushed for the door, the flashing sword in his left hand carving a path.

Outside he paused, momentarily dazzled by the sunlight reflected on the snow. But knowing that pursuit was just behind him, he stumbled down the steps of the temple as quickly as he could.

Matsuzo's voice sounded close by. "Kongomaru! What are you doing here?"

Now that Zenta's eyes were accustomed to the glare, he saw that Matsuzo was trying to unfasten the leash tethering Kongomaru to a tree.

"Leave that dog alone!" said Zenta. "He's vicious, and he'll attack you if you let him loose."

There was a clatter followed by angry cries as Ryutaro and his men, also dazzled by the sun, jostled each other on the steps.

"We can handle those men," said Matsuzo confidently. He patted the dog, who was snarling and straining at his leash. "You'll fight for us, won't you, Kongomaru?"

"Stop fooling with that dog and listen to me!" snapped Zenta. "We're no match for that crowd because my right hand is injured and useless. And that dog isn't going to fight on our side. He's the one who attacked me!"

As he finished speaking, Zenta became aware of two things. Ryutaro and his men had not rushed forward to attack them. They were frozen on the steps of the temple, staring with consternation at a motionless figure in front of the pine trees at the edge of the clearing. Kongomaru's barking increased its fury, and Zenta finally realized that the dog was not barking at him, but at the new arrival.

The figure was clothed all in black, with a black hood that completely covered his face except for the eyes. The corners of the hood stood up, like the pointed ears of an animal. The very stillness of the figure suggested the stillness of a wild beast about to spring. Zenta knew he was looking at the Cat.

He cast a quick glance at Ryutaro and his men and saw that they were terrified. Ryutaro may earlier have entertained thoughts of plotting against the Cat, but he was completely cowed into submission now.

Zenta made his decision. He was certain that if he were to fight the Cat, he would need both hands and all his skills. Now he had to retreat. "Run!" he shouted to Matsuzo.

At that instant Matsuzo managed to undo the knot tying Kongomaru to the tree. The dog lunged toward the black figure, and Matsuzo, who had wound his hand around Kongomaru's leash, was nearly pulled off his feet.

"Run!" urged Zenta again. "We have to escape!"

"Not without Kongomaru," panted Matsuzo, straining to pull the dog back.

"How many times do I have to tell you—" began Zenta. Then he saw to his amazement that the dog was actually responding to Matsuzo's command. For some reason Kongomaru had decided to obey the young ronin. As they ran through the woods, the dog turned a few times to snarl back, but he had apparently chosen his friends and was staying with them.

8

"They don't seem to be after us," Matsuzo said. The two ronin stopped and listened. It was true. There were no sounds of pursuit.

"The Cat doesn't know how far he can trust Ryutaro," said Zenta. "Right now I suspect Ryutaro is engaged in some difficult explaining. That's probably what's delaying the pursuit."

Now that there was no need to run, they could talk. Matsuzo listened astonished as Zenta told him about Ryutaro's proposal. "And I was so sure that the peddlers were the ones who were committing the murders!" he said.

"The impression I got was that many of the peddlers were disturbed by the murders but were too frightened of the Cat to stop him," said Zenta. "I suppose that's why Ryutaro was trying to get my help."

"I wonder how the Cat found out that Ryutaro was plotting against him?" said Matsuzo.

"One of the men must have reported to him," said Zenta. "I saw a man there who looked like a Buddhist priest. He got up and left while I was there, so he may have been the informer. Ryutaro said he posed as an exorcist."

"I've already heard about this so-called exorcist," Matsuzo said. After a while he asked, "Do you think Ryutaro will go back to working for the Cat, then?"

"I'm afraid so," said Zenta. "If I had been more clever, I would have pretended to cooperate with him so that we could work together against the Cat. But I was so disgusted by the way those peddlers terrorized the people here—even Ikken—that I couldn't hide my feelings or pretend to accept Ryutaro's offer."

They were out of the bamboo grove and saw the houses of the village a short distance in front of them. Matsuzo loosened his hold on Kongomaru, who bounded ahead, obviously enjoying his freedom. The young ronin relaxed. For the time being they seemed to be safe from the Cat and the band of peddlers. The wind even changed direction and blew behind them as if gently urging them toward the safety of the houses.

Suddenly Kongomaru stopped, turned his head, and sniffed. Then without warning he lunged at Zenta, who flung out his arms to defend his face.

Matsuzo struggled to pull Kongomaru back, but the dog had his jaws tightly clamped on Zenta's wrist. Only after repeated commands did he succeed in persuading Kongomaru to let go.

Matsuzo wound the leash again tightly about his hand. "Why did you attack Zenta, Kongomaru?" he asked reproachfully. "Can't you tell that he's a friend?"

He turned to look anxiously at Zenta, who was sitting on the ground cradling his right arm. "Did he hurt you?" Matsuzo asked.

Zenta did not reply at first. He finally took a deep breath and raised his head. "One of these days I might do something drastic to that dog, even if he is Asa's protector."

"He doesn't seem to like you," Matsuzo said weakly. Kongomaru continued to growl and pull at the leash.

"I don't like him very much either," retorted Zenta. "But I don't try to bite him every time we meet!"

Matsuzo was completely baffled. Kongomaru was a very intelligent dog, he was convinced of that. Then why did he make this vicious attack on Zenta, who had done nothing to provoke him? "Let me see your hand," Matsuzo said.

At the sight of Zenta's swollen and angry wrist Matsuzo winced. "Did Kongomaru do that just now?"

"Not all of it," Zenta said shortly. "The black and blue marks underneath are his earlier work."

Matsuzo turned to Kongomaru and coaxed him patiently. Finally the dog's fury subsided and he came over and nuzzled the young ronin affectionately.

"Kongomaru seems to like *me*," said Matsuzo, feeling puzzled but unable to prevent himself from sounding smug.

"You probably feed him," said Zenta. "I noticed that he was friendly with Ryutaro, who gave him treats. That dog is so stupid and greedy that he makes friends with anyone who hands out food."

That was exactly what Hirobei had said earlier, but Matsuzo refused to be convinced. "Well, Kongomaru does like to eat. A big, active dog like this needs lots of nourishment."

"I still say the dog is stupid," insisted Zenta. "He can't tell the difference between friend and foe."

"That's not true!" protested Matsuzo. He patted Kongomaru, who pressed close, the very picture of loyalty and devotion.

The two men exchanged information as they walked toward the village. Matsuzo told Zenta about the piece of cloth he had picked up and about what had happened during his visit to Asa's house that morning. When he finished he said, "So you see, Kongomaru knew that the Cat was the enemy. He barked at that figure in black at the peddlers' hideout just now. That must have been the Cat!"

A sudden thought struck him. "Wait! I just realized something: Kongomaru attacked you right after the wind changed. He must have caught a whiff of something belonging to the enemy. When you came up to the Cat last night, did he leave a trace of something on you?"

"You may be right!" said Zenta. He immediately began to examine his clothes. Matsuzo helped him, but they could find nothing beyond the rips that always appeared regularly in Zenta's clothes. Some of the tears were Kongomaru's recent contributions. The two men finally decided that if there was anything, only the sensitive nose of a dog could detect it.

"I still think that I was never that close to the Cat last night," muttered Zenta.

At a fork in the road Matsuzo stopped. "Where should we go first?"

"To Asa's house," replied Zenta. "I want to meet Hirobei."

"Why?" asked Matsuzo, surprised. "He's just the business manager for Asa's grandfather. The only thing he knows about is money."

"That's exactly what I want to discuss with him," said Zenta. "One of Ryutaro's men said that the Cat has some plan to get hold of the fortune that Asa's grandfather is leaving to her. I don't like the sound of it at all, and I'm hoping that Hirobei can tell me more about the money."

So the Cat was interested in money, thought Matsuzo. That made him sound more like a human being than a supernatural monster, but no less sinister.

Asa's house was a little distance from the village proper. When they came in sight of the big house with its high fence, Matsuzo slipped off Kongomaru's leash, and the dog broke into a run.

Kongomaru's barks soon brought the gatekeeper. "There you are, you naughty dog!" said the gatekeeper, opening the gate. "The young mistress has been looking all over for you!"

On seeing the two ronin approach he bowed deeply. But when Zenta asked to see Hirobei, the gatekeeper replied that the merchant had left a while ago and was not expected back immediately. Would they like to see the mistress or her daughter?

To Matsuzo's disappointment Zenta declined. As they turned away from the house he said, "I don't want to alarm Asa. She would probably collapse from fright if we ask her about the Cat's plot."

Zenta had a low opinion of Asa's spirit. Matsuzo knew that his friend admired women with courage. After the way Asa had cringed at the mere mention of the Cat, Zenta had probably dismissed the girl as timid and feeble.

"We could talk to Toshi, Asa's mother," suggested Matsuzo. "I didn't have the impression that she frightens easily."

Zenta shook his head. "No, but she doesn't like us. I don't think it's anything personal: she just dislikes the warrior class. And there is something else . . . " He hesitated.

"What? You mean she wouldn't help even to protect her own daughter?" asked Matsuzo, shocked.

"No . . . " Zenta said slowly. "But I did wonder why Asa's grandfather would leave his fortune to his granddaughter, and not to his daughter. It would be a touchy subject to bring up with Toshi."

"Then where should we go now?" asked Matsuzo.

"There is one person who might have information," said Zenta. "Ikken. His brother was married to Toshi."

"But that means we'll have to mention the peddlers," said Matsuzo. "I thought we don't want to bring that up with him. Since he's one of the extortion victims, it would be humiliating for him."

"That can't be helped," said Zenta. "It was foolish of

me to think that we can avoid the subject with Ikken. The danger to Asa and others is too great."

They found Ikken's house different. The snow had been swept from the paths with a coarse twig broom. Since there were no servants, Matsuzo knew that the work had been done by Ikken himself. The careful swirls of the broom had been made by a man who found beauty even in an everyday task.

Most of the heavy wooden shutters had been removed, and a few of the sliding doors stood open to let air and light into the house. The feeling of brooding melancholy and desolation was gone.

Ikken himself seemed different. When they went in to greet him, he smiled at them with what seemed like genuine welcome. "Young men are always hungry," he said, and the look he gave Zenta was affectionate. "Go and eat first. Later there is something I want to discuss with you." The words were almost the same as the ones he had used last night, but there was a new warmth in the way he said them.

In the kitchen Matsuzo stared at the pile of empty boxes. "We're not the only hungry ones," he couldn't help saying. At this rate the food they had brought wouldn't last through the New Year's festival.

Zenta looked perplexed as well. "Two people have been eating here," he said, pointing to the chopsticks and bowls.

For a moment Matsuzo wondered if one of the peddlers had come to make demands for more money. But if so, Ikken wouldn't have offered him food. Someone could have come to pay a New Year's call—Asa, for example, or her mother Toshi. It could even have been Hirobei. After all, the merchant had looked after the business interests of Ikken's brother.

The two ronin opened a few more boxes of prepared cold food. "Some hot soup would be nice," said Zenta. "Do you know how to make it?"

"Let me see. You boil water," suggested Matsuzo helpfully. They got the wood stove going well and placed a pan of water on top. After that they were at a loss.

"I think some seaweed would add a nice flavor," said Matsuzo. He found a curly strip of dried seaweed, white with powdered salt. "Shall I put the whole thing in?" he asked doubtfully. The strip was as long as his arm. He didn't remember ever seeing a strip of seaweed as long as his arm in a soup bowl.

"How can you be so silly?" exclaimed Zenta. "Break it into small pieces, of course!"

That was easy to say, but hard to perform, Matsuzo thought as he wrestled with the tough, elastic strip of seaweed. He took out his sword.

"You can't use your sword to cut food!" cried Zenta in a shocked voice. "Wait, let me find something to cut it with."

He rummaged around and suddenly held up something which looked like a short, stubby stick with pointed ends. "Look! I've found a piece of dried fish. It's supposed to make good soup." He dropped it into the pan of water with a splash.

"Are you sure you should put the whole thing in?" asked Matsuzo. "I thought you shave off little bits of it for soup stock. It's supposed to be very expensive. Ikken may have to make it last for months."

Zenta looked guilty. "Maybe we can fish it out afterward, dry it, and use it again."

The two men soon got tired of waiting for the soup to boil and decided to start eating. They had found more clean dishes and chopsticks, which meant that they had enough to last for a few more meals without washing. As they ate, Matsuzo noticed that Zenta was having trouble using his chopsticks. "How long will it take before you can use your right hand again?" he asked.

Before Zenta could reply, the soup boiled over and fell hissing into the fire. Matsuzo grabbed the hot pan but dropped it immediately and yelled with pain. Most of the soup spilled, putting out the fire altogether.

When Matsuzo eventually poured out his share of the soup, it came to about two mouthfuls. They finished eating, and as Matsuzo put away the dirty dishes to join the others in the cupboard, he said, "The soup didn't taste too bad, what there was of it, but I don't think it was worth the trouble. I've heard of people getting married for the sake of having a bowl of hot soup every evening."

"That's too heavy a price to pay for soup," said Zenta.

Matsuzo knew the reason for Zenta's cynical attitude toward women. He had once been attracted to a beautiful and fascinating woman, only to discover almost too late that she was a murderess. Zenta never spoke her name again, but Matsuzo knew that the hurt had been a deep one.

Nevertheless Matsuzo felt it only just to point out that

some women had attractions besides their ability to make soup. "That girl Asa might make someone a good wife," he remarked.

Ikken said almost the same thing a little later when Zenta went to visit him in his room. The tea master delicately questioned Zenta to discover if he had matrimonial commitments. On discovering that he had none, Ikken looked relieved. "Asa is a good girl and is of an age to be married," he began.

Zenta was embarrassed, for he could see what was coming. To put off the moment he said, "I understand that she was to have married Shunken."

The tea master's face went rigid, and Zenta saw that his mention of Shunken had been a mistake. Ikken said harshly, "Shunken is dead. We will speak no more of him." After a few painful seconds he said, "However, there is still the question of Asa's future. The girl's grandfather has said that because of the betrothal, I am in a sense Asa's father-in-law and therefore should have a say in planning for her. Toshi, her mother, has also agreed to abide by any decision I make on Asa's marriage."

From Ikken's expression, Zenta guessed that Toshi's agreement had been given grudgingly. Of course, there was very little she could do.

"The question of Asa's future is complicated," continued Ikken. "There is a large amount of money involved, since her grandfather is enormously rich."

That was the opening Zenta needed. He was glad that Ikken had brought up the subject first. "Then Asa, not her mother, is the heiress to the fortune?" he asked.

Ikken misunderstood the reason for Zenta's interest. He said, "Asa will inherit most of the money. If you take her for your wife, her money will be extremely useful in case you have ambitious plans."

"Oh, no, I couldn't do that!" exclaimed Zenta. He immediately realized that he had spoken more bluntly than tactfully. The thought of settling down with a rich wife was stifling. "Sensei, the life I have chosen has no use for money," he tried to explain.

Something was badly wrong, he thought. The tea ceremony, as Ikken practiced it, was the very embodiment of frugality and simplicity. That he should urge Zenta to marry Asa for her money was incomprehensible.

The tea master was clearly disappointed by Zenta's refusal. "What about your friend, then?" asked Ikken. "He looks like a well-bred young man and should make the girl happy."

Zenta thought that Asa might be too quiet for Matsuzo, who liked girls with more sparkle and vivacity. But he remembered that only a short while ago Matsuzo had said that Asa would make a fine wife. "I'll speak to him about it, if you like," he told Ikken.

The tea master nodded. "I feel a responsibility toward the girl, and her inheritance makes the responsibility a heavy burden. Her grandfather is a merchant who made his fortune doing business not only with wealthy warlords, but even with foreigners from across the seas."

The turbulent age in which they lived had seen great suffering among the victims of the wars, but it had also seen unprecedented social changes. As a class, the merchants had always been despised by the warriors. It was a time of great opportunities, however, and those merchants who had initiative managed to acquire both wealth and power. Zenta had met some of the new breed of merchant, whose influence was greater than that of many warlords. If Asa's grandfather was one of these, her fortune would be a sizable one.

Nevertheless, Zenta could not quite see Matsuzo as a merchant. His young friend had a touch of snobbishness and was very proud of his lineage. "Would Asa's husband have to give up his samurai status and be adopted by her grandfather?" Zenta asked.

He saw too late that his question had been tactless. In marrying Asa's mother, Ikken's own brother had become a merchant. But the tea master showed no displeasure at Zenta's question. Perhaps the hurt had healed long ago. "Asa's husband could remain a samurai if he wished," he replied. "Her grandfather has retired from business, having made enough money for his ambitions. He is fond of his granddaughter and wants to see her well married."

"She is a lovely girl," said Zenta. "If Matsuzo married her, he would be a fortunate man."

Ikken looked pleased. "In looks Asa resembles my brother. As for her education, I've done the best I could to teach her a few accomplishments I considered important. She writes an excellent hand and seems to have a natural talent for the tea ceremony. Best of all, she has a good understanding of what is required to be the wife of a samurai."

The tea master paused for a moment and then said, "There is just one thing I should mention. If Asa should die before she marries, then all the money goes to her mother, Toshi. And if Toshi remarries, her husband will have control of the fortune."

"Why doesn't Toshi's father leave the money to her in the first place?" asked Zenta.

Ikken's face showed a trace of amusement. "Her father, the merchant, is a social climber. He thought that he could form a suitable alliance by marrying Toshi to my brother. After my brother died Toshi's father wanted her to marry into another samurai family, but she refused." For an instant Ikken's contempt for his sister-in-law showed. "She told her father that she preferred to marry a merchant—someone like Hirobei, her father's business manager."

Toshi, forced by her father to marry into a family that despised her, must have had an unhappy marriage. Zenta could now understand her hostility toward the warrior class.

"Since his daughter has defied him," continued Ikken, "the merchant has placed all his hopes on his grand-daughter, Asa. He wants to see the girl make a good marriage, and to improve her chances he is settling his fortune on her."

Zenta knew that it was time to speak of his fears. "Sensei, I've heard some alarming rumors today. I fell in with a band of medicine peddlers, and they were talking about one of their leaders, someone called the Cat, taking possession of Asa's fortune."

Again the dread was in Ikken's eyes. "Why do you listen to idle talk?" he said angrily.

Stubbornly Zenta went on. "These people are utterly unscrupulous, and we must protect Asa from them. Can you tell me anything about the Cat?"

Ikken turned away and refused to look at Zenta. "I can't tell you anything!"

"Sensei, Asa may be in great danger!" For the first time in his life Zenta found himself challenging the tea master and he didn't enjoy it.

"If those ruffians are dangerous, why don't you do something about them?" said Ikken. His voice shook and his face was white.

Zenta found his teacher's distress unbearable to watch. It was useless to probe further. He would have to find a way to fight the Cat and Ryutaro's men without Ikken's help.

The tea master breathed deeply for a while, and when he spoke his voice was much quieter. "This is not how I want to celebrate your return. Come, let's have tea and calm ourselves."

Zenta wanted to shout, "How can we afford to spend time for tea? There are terrible dangers threatening!"

But self-discipline was what he had learned in this room, and he followed Ikken to the corner of the study used for the tea ceremony. As he watched the tea master's deliberate, unhurried motions, he realized that Ikken, who had been even more disturbed than he was, had already brought himself under control. Zenta exerted himself to achieve an equal calm.

Since the tea master had not made preparations in advance for tea, he started by getting the fire ready. He lifted the iron kettle from the sunken hearth and began to mold the ashes into a pleasing shape. Zenta saw that Ikken's hands were perfectly steady. When Ikken was satisfied with the shape of the molded ash, he sprinkled a little additional wet ash and said, "We'll use the last of the incense that Shunken liked."

From the charcoal basket the tea master first took a large piece of charcoal and put it into the hearth. With as much care as if arranging flowers, he placed smaller pieces of charcoal over the main piece until the hearth became a work of art in itself. All the charcoal had been fired and sawed by Ikken's own hands.

Zenta stared at the charcoal basket, his thoughts racing. The basket now being used by Ikken was only a cheap one, but earlier that day he had seen a beautiful charcoal basket that had looked familiar. Now he knew why. That basket used to be Ikken's. It had disappeared, along with most of the other valuables of the tea master, only to reappear at the peddlers' hideout. The charcoal in it, too, was special. The monk who acted as exorcist for the peddler band had taken away the charcoal, saying that it was his.

At last Zenta knew how the peddlers had induced fainting spells in the girls of the village.

9

"The trick is to use Ikken's special charcoal," Zenta told Matsuzo, "charcoal he had refined himself so that it gave almost no smell when it burned."

After the tea ceremony, Zenta had joined Matsuzo, and the two men were sitting in their room polishing their swords. As they worked Zenta explained his theory on how the peddlers had managed to induce fainting spells.

"Ikken was very particular about incense during the tea ceremony," continued Zenta. "Like many tea masters, he was a great expert on incense. He used to tell me that the dusty smell of ordinary charcoal interfered with his enjoyment of incense. After years of experimenting, he perfected a special kind of charcoal so pure that it was odorless."

"How did the peddlers get possession of it?" asked Matsuzo.

Zenta's mouth tightened and he rubbed his sword angrily. "I suspect it was when Ikken had to sell his more valuable tea utensils, and the peddlers must have picked up some of the pieces from a local trader. Or maybe Ryutaro's men simply took possession of the pieces directly. This morning when I was at the hideout, I recognized Ikken's charcoal basket there."

Matsuzo still didn't see how the special charcoal could cause faintness. "Why wasn't Ikken affected by fainting spells when he used the charcoal, then?"

"If used *normally*," said Zenta, "this special charcoal is no more harmful than ordinary charcoal."

Matsuzo frowned. "Then I don't understand—"

"Think!" said Zenta. "What does the exorcist ask the family to do when they are terrified of the Cat?"

"They are told to seal all the windows and doors at night to keep out evil spirits," said Matsuzo slowly. "I'm beginning to see now. The air becomes poisonous from charcoal fumes. . . ."

"Yes, the air becomes poisonous and makes people dizzy," said Zenta. "Normally people realize the danger when the room becomes heavy with the smell of charcoal. But if the brazier contains the specially refined charcoal —probably put there by the 'helpful' exorcist—then there is no warning when the air gets bad."

"It all fits," said Matsuzo. "The parents then become alarmed by these fainting spells and rush out to buy medicine from the peddlers."

"And if they don't buy the medicine, their daughter is killed by the Cat," said Zenta. "Except that in the case of Jiro's daughter, the medicine didn't do any good.

It's the first break between the Cat and the peddler band."

Matsuzo thought back to the first two victims. "How did the peddlers manage the charcoal trick with the girls whose parents didn't call in the exorcist?"

"According to what I heard, the first two girls didn't suffer from dizziness," replied Zenta. "Those girls were murdered by the Cat before the peddlers came. All the talk about fainting fits came later."

Matsuzo tried to recall everything he had heard from Hirobei concerning the murders, and he decided that Zenta was right. The Cat had begun to work with the peddlers only after the first two murders had already been committed.

He looked up from his polishing to find Zenta regarding him with a faintly embarrassed expression. "I haven't had much practice as a matchmaker," Zenta began. Then he continued in a rush, "How would you like to marry Asa?"

"Marry Asa?" said Matsuzo. His voice came out as a squeak. "Did Ikken suggest that?"

"Well, yes. She is a very pretty girl, she has charming manners, and she will inherit an enormous amount of money."

"And her husband will have to become a merchant," said Matsuzo in disgust.

"No, he won't," said Zenta quickly. "If you marry her, you can continue your life as a samurai. Just think, you'll have hot soup every day without burning your fingers."

"How can I continue my present life as a ronin and

still have hot soup every day?" demanded Matsuzo. "You're not suggesting that we take her along?"

"Don't be silly! You won't be wandering around as a ronin any longer. You'll become respectable."

Matsuzo thought about some of the girls he had met, one or two in particular with bright eyes and ready wit. "No, Asa is an attractive girl, but she's too quiet for me. I'd die of boredom within a week."

Zenta sighed. "That's a pity. Asa is almost a daughter to Ikken, and he wants to see her safely married."

"If that's the case, why don't you marry her yourself?" retorted Matsuzo. "After all, he is *your* teacher."

When Zenta refused to meet his eye, Matsuzo became suspicious. "Ikken first suggested that you marry Asa, didn't he? And you refused?"

The two men looked at each other, and suddenly both burst out laughing. "I did refuse," confessed Zenta. "And I think my main reason was fear of boredom, too."

Now it was Matsuzo's turn to persuade. "You don't have to stay home. You can use Asa's money to buy arms, hire men, and do something ambitious instead of just wandering from place to place, living on the edge of starvation."

Zenta's face turned sober and he shook his head. "I don't have any ambitions that require Asa's money. Besides, money turns people cautious. Once they become rich they want to spend all their time guarding their money."

"You may not have ambitions requiring Asa's money, but someone else does," Matsuzo pointed out.

"Yes. One reason why Ikken wants to have Asa married

quickly, I think, is to prevent the Cat's getting possession of her fortune."

"Did Ikken . . . did you warn him about the dangers?"

"I didn't have to warn him," said Zenta shortly. "He already knew. But he refused to discuss it with me."

Matsuzo could tell that Zenta had been hurt by Ikken's refusal to confide in him. "What shall we do, then? We can't just sit doing nothing."

For some minutes the two men worked silently. Then Zenta suddenly sheathed his swords and stood up. He seemed to have come to a decision. "I think we had better go back to Asa's house."

Having made up his mind, Zenta seemed impatient to leave. He would not even stop to tell Ikken of his intentions, and when Matsuzo questioned him about this, his response was curt. Matsuzo knew that Zenta idolized his teacher and realized that the tea master's abject fear of the peddlers was a great disappointment to him.

Outside, the sun was already low and the short winter day would not last much longer. The long shadows cast by the trees looked blue and sinister on the snow. As he walked Matsuzo felt all his senses becoming more alert. He swept his eyes over the hillside and caught a flicker of bamboo leaves to the right above him.

Zenta checked his stride momentarily, but then continued as if nothing had happened. "Ambush," he said softly. "Watch your right side."

Matsuzo tried to keep his expression casual. "What shall we do? Will you be able to use your right hand?"

"No, but it's too late to turn back now," said Zenta.

"At least I have a good idea where they intend to attack us. After the next bend in the path, there's a wide stretch where they can place several men. I suspect they'll also have a couple of men on the hill above the road so they can rush down on us from behind."

It turned out almost exactly as Zenta had predicted. Three of the peddlers stood blocking the path, their swords out and their faces grinning in anticipation.

Matsuzo threw a quick glance to the side and saw three other men crouched on the hill. Neither Ryutaro nor the Cat had taken the trouble to come, apparently confident that underlings would easily overcome a man with a disabled hand and an inexperienced youngster. Matsuzo felt insulted, but he quickly suppressed his anger. It would only make him careless.

One of the peddlers ran forward, and at Zenta's nod Matsuzo stepped up to meet him. Noticing that the man held his sword a little high, Matsuzo decided on an upward cut. His sword flashed out and up before the attacker even began his downward stroke. As the peddler fell, Matsuzo gave him a push, sending him toppling down the hill. His last glimpse of the peddler's face showed the mouth open in astonishment.

A second man moved forward. He was more cautious than the first, the confident grin on his face having been wiped off by the fate of his comrade.

"Shall I take this one, too?" asked Matsuzo.

"Why not?" said Zenta indifferently.

His indifference goaded the peddler into carelessness. Matsuzo sidestepped the hasty attack and struck before his opponent could turn around.

There was a rustle as one of the watchers above them came rushing down the steep slope. Zenta stood firm and simply held the scabbard of his sword straight out, a little distance above the ground. The man saw the danger, but it was too late to check himself or change direction. Hurtling down the hill at great speed, he tripped over Zenta's sword and somersaulted across the path. Down the other side he went, and finally crashed into a tree.

Matsuzo barely had time to observe this before he had to meet the attack of the third man on the path. This man was more cautious than the other two and a far more skilled swordsman. Matsuzo used everything he had learned from Zenta before he succeeded in cutting down this opponent.

That left the two men on the hill. Recovering his breath Matsuzo shouted, "Come down and join your friends!"

"But do be careful of your step," suggested Zenta. "It's slippery."

Matsuzo could hear agitated whispers. The two men above them were probably discussing whether it would be more dangerous to go down and meet the two ronin or to go back and report failure to their leaders. Apparently they decided that the second course would be less fatal, for they turned and scrambled up the hill.

Matsuzo laughed as he watched the men stumble and slip in their haste. "Well. Now they know that I'm not such a contemptible opponent after all."

Zenta grinned. "You have an innocent, childlike look

that's better than a dozen tricks of swordsmanship. People tend to underestimate you until it's too late."

A groan came from the man who had been stunned by his collision with the tree, and he began to stir. Zenta turned him over with his foot. "What shall we do with this fellow? Put him out of his misery?"

Matsuzo was surprised, for Zenta never indulged in casual killing. Then he caught Zenta's eye and understood. "Why not? The man is useless. Unless you think he can give us some information?"

The peddler sat up eagerly. "Don't kill me! I'll tell you everything I know!" He crouched down in front of Zenta and bowed his forehead into the muddy slush and snow.

"Why isn't Ryutaro here at the ambush?" asked Zenta. "Does he think that I can't do any more fighting with my bad hand?"

"That's what Ryutaro told the Cat," said the peddler. "But some of us think he's still hoping you will change your mind and join forces with him. That's why he isn't part of the ambush."

"Why didn't the Cat join the ambush?" asked Matsuzo. "He thought we were so insignificant that he couldn't be bothered to come?"

"The Cat told Ryutaro that he had important business," said the peddler and paused.

"What business?" demanded Matsuzo impatiently.

"I . . . I don't know," stammered the peddler.

"Yes, you do," said Matsuzo. "Or you can make a good guess."

The peddler had the look of an animal caught in a trap. Finally he said, "I heard the Cat say that your arrival had upset his plans, and he had to move forward his whole campaign against the heiress."

Matsuzo felt a touch of coldness. He saw that Zenta had tensed. "What do you mean by our arrival upsetting his plans?" asked Zenta. His voice was quiet, but there was danger in his face.

The peddler licked his lips. "The Cat learned that you might marry the heiress, and so he had to get to her first."

Before Matsuzo realized what was happening, Zenta had turned and was plunging down the hill along the narrow foot path. Matsuzo looked back briefly to see the peddler running away from them as fast as he could. Hurrying after Zenta Matsuzo thought over the peddler's disturbing words. Somehow the Cat had learned of Ikken's wish to have Asa marry himself or Zenta. It meant that the Cat had a close knowledge of Asa's family affairs.

Keeping a wary eye for further attacks, they hurried as fast as they could on the icy path. There were no more attempts at ambush. "Ryutaro seems to be saving his men for something else," said Zenta. "I'm not sure that I like that."

By the time they arrived at the open plain around the village, dusk was approaching. In the softer light the scene looked rustic and peaceful. Matsuzo could even hear the sound of a drum in the distance, probably some local New Year's celebration. When he saw Asa's house, he relaxed. The walls were intact; the house looked untouched.

The gatekeeper was cheerful and flushed, presumably full of New Year's refreshments. As the two ronin entered the gate he positively groveled and left immediately to inform his mistress of their arrival.

Toshi appeared, and as they exchanged New Year's greetings Matsuzo noticed that her manner had become much pleasanter. For such a cold, self-possessed woman she sounded almost cordial.

"Thank you for honoring our house with your visit," she said, bowing low to Zenta. "We didn't have the opportunity to greet you when we called on my brother-in-law this morning."

Zenta was also startled by the change in Toshi's manner. "It's very peaceful here," he said, looking around the courtyard.

On New Year's Day one would expect the house to be thronged with callers, village people, or business associates of Toshi's father. The quiet in the house was unnatural.

"There were plenty of callers here when I came this morning," said Matsuzo, puzzled.

Toshi laughed nervously. "That's true. We had the usual number of callers this morning, but in the course of the afternoon people stopped coming. It's as if the news has spread that we have a dangerous disease in the house."

That would explain Toshi's nervousness and unexpected cordiality. Since it was obligatory to pay New

Year's calls on one's superiors, a family's social standing could be measured by the number of people who came to call. Small wonder that Toshi was uneasy when her stream of visitors had trickled to a stop. By now she was delighted to see any visitors, even samurai.

As the two men followed Toshi up into the main reception room of the house, the door opposite them opened and Hirobei entered, rubbing his hands briskly. More polite greetings and bowing had to take place before all the requirements of etiquette were satisfied.

Finally Toshi looked at her business manager. "Where have you been all day?"

"I've been paying New Year's calls," the merchant answered carelessly. "I also had some business, but I'll tell you about it later."

He turned, and his cynical eyes with their droopy lids were penetrating as they examined Zenta. "I've heard of your reputation, sir. It's a great privilege to meet you at last."

Zenta was looking at Hirobei with equal curiosity. "I was also looking forward to meeting you. There are some things that I'd like to discuss with you."

"I see that you've hurt your hand!" exclaimed the merchant. "How bad is it?"

Zenta held out his hand. It was black and blue and puffy around the teeth marks. "I had a little misunderstanding with Kongomaru," he confessed.

Toshi hissed with shock, and Hirobei exclaimed angrily, "That stupid dog again! There is no explaining his behavior! Toshi, you'll have to get rid of him before he kills someone."

"But Asa—" began Toshi.

"We'll have to think of some other way to protect Asa," interrupted Hirobei.

"In fact it's about Asa's safety that we came," said Zenta.

It was then that everyone noticed something odd: Asa had not appeared to greet the New Year's guests, as was her duty.

10

Toshi frowned. She went to the door and summoned a maidservant. "Do you know where the young mistress is?" she asked the girl.

The maid looked puzzled. "Didn't she tell you, Madame? She went to visit Kiku, the younger daughter of Jiro the carpenter."

Panic made Matsuzo's voice sharp. "Why did she do a foolhardy thing like that? Doesn't she know that there are dangerous men in the village?"

The maid shrank back in alarm and looked ready to take flight. Toshi answered for her. "Asa is friendly with the girl. There is no one in the village who is really suitable company for my daughter, but Kiku is unusually bright and Asa took an interest in her. Perhaps she went over to the girl's house to console the family."

"The young mistress received a message saying that the girl had some secret information about her older sister's murder," said the maid. "She was afraid to give it to anyone else."

"Do you mean to say that Asa went alone?" cried Matsuzo.

"She took Kongomaru with her," said the maid, ready to weep. She looked at her mistress and said, "I thought you knew."

"I wouldn't call Kongomaru exactly reliable," said Zenta.

"Kongomaru is completely loyal to Asa!" said Toshi. "You samurai are not the only ones capable of loyalty."

"I agree with Zenta," said Hirobei. "Kongomaru is not only stupid, he runs off to anyone who gives him food."

Zenta stood up. "Asa may be in danger. We have to find her."

Toshi turned pale. "You . . . you said that you came to talk about Asa's safety. Is there any reason to think that she's threatened particularly?"

There was no need to alarm her until they were sure that the news was really bad. The story about the Cat's plot to gain possession of Asa's money could wait. Zenta said merely, "It's not good for a young girl to venture out these days."

As he and Matsuzo hurried to the door, Hirobei jumped up after them. "I'll show you the way to Jiro's house."

"That's not necessary," said Zenta. "I've been there already. I know where it is."

While the two ronin were putting on their shoes at the front entrance, they heard the sound of drumming coming from outside the walls of Toshi's house. Grinning broadly the gatekeeper rushed to the gate and opened it to admit two lion dancers and their drummer.

As word of their arrival went around, the servants began coming into the front courtyard to watch the spectacle. Toshi looked worriedly down at the milling scene. "That's strange. We haven't had any lion dancing in this village for several years. Now they're starting again. I'll have to bring out refreshments and find some money for the dancers."

The lion dance was so much a part of the New Year's celebrations that soon all of Toshi's household crowded into the courtyard. The two ronin had difficulty forcing their way to the gate through the packed spectators.

Looking at the energetic hopping and shaking of the dancers, Matsuzo couldn't remember when he had seen a more dilapidated lion. The large carved wooden lion's head was weather-beaten and the paint on the eyeballs had peeled, making the round, bulging eyes look blind. The lower jaw of the huge, grinning mouth hung slack, which gave the lion a drunken, dissipated look. To make matters worse, the green and white draperies over the arms and shoulders of the dancers were in tatters. What the props lacked in elegance, however, the two dancers made up by enthusiasm, especially the head dancer.

"We haven't had the lion dance in our village since the Vampire Cat curse started," one of the servants remarked.

"Yes, and the dancers are badly out of practice," said another. "Look at that head dancer. He's trying to be energetic, but he's only clumsy."

The tempo of the drumming speeded up and the dancers became more and more frenzied. They ended finally with a stamping of feet and collapsed in a bow to the spectators. The crowd, applauding the spirit rather than the quality of the dancing, shouted out their appreciation.

At a sign from Toshi serving girls brought out dishes of food and an iron kettle of heated *toso*, the special New Year's drink made of spiced, sweet sake. The drummer and the young boy who danced the tail half of the lion eagerly fell on the refreshments.

Matsuzo noticed that the head dancer still kept the mask over his face. He was wondering about this when he felt a touch on his arm. "We've wasted too much time already," said Zenta. "Let's hurry."

As the two ronin moved toward the gate, the head dancer quickly approached them. "I have something to tell you, sir," he whispered to Zenta. While the attention of the others in the courtyard was on the refreshments, the dancer raised his mask and lifted the cloth drapery.

Matsuzo stared with astonishment at the tavern keeper. "What are you doing here? You're not a lion dancer!"

"I came to warn you," whispered the tavern keeper. "Ryutaro's men are stationed at all the approaches to this house."

"So that was it," said Zenta. "We ran into one party on our way here from Ikken's house."

"Now that it's getting dark," said the tavern keeper, "the peddlers are showing themselves and coming forward to tighten the circle around the house. The villagers are so frightened by the sight of all these armed peddlers that they're afraid to venture out and pay New Year's calls."

"But *you* came," said Matsuzo.

The tavern keeper hoisted the lion's head with a swagger. "I'm not afraid of a bunch of quack medicine peddlers!"

"Didn't anyone try to stop you?" asked Zenta.

"I'd thought of that," said the tavern keeper. "Since you and I were seen together this morning, the peddlers might recognize me as your assistant. So I hit on the idea of using a lion dancer disguise. The equipment has been stored at my house ever since the last lion dancer owed me money for his drinks."

The man was worse than a pawnbroker, thought Matsuzo indignantly, thinking of Zenta's ivory figurine also in his greedy grasp.

"I made my errand boy take up the back half of the lion, while I became the front half. None of the peddlers tried to stop me. In fact they laughed and cheered me on."

"I wonder if Ryutaro is under the impression that Asa is here at the house," said Zenta. "She and her dog have gone to visit Jiro the carpenter."

"The girl is not at Jiro's house," said the tavern keeper. "When I was under the lion's mask, I overheard one of the peddlers saying that she was waiting alone in an abandoned house at the end of the street. It belonged to the family of one of the other murdered girls, but they moved away after her death, and the house is deserted now."

The news chilled Matsuzo. It was much worse than he had thought. "What possessed Asa to go there?"

"I don't like the sound of this," said Zenta grimly, making for the gate.

The tavern keeper grasped his sleeve. "Wait! Ryutaro knows you are here, and his men won't let anyone through. As soon as it gets dark they plan to attack this place."

"What do you think?" Matsuzo asked Zenta. "Can we fight our way through?"

Zenta looked at his injured hand and considered. Suddenly he smiled. "We can get through in the same way the tavern keeper did, by pretending to be lion dancers. I'll be the head of the lion and you can be the tail."

"What!" cried Matsuzo. "I've never tried anything like that in my life!"

The tavern keeper grinned. "Neither have I, but I was pretty good, wasn't I?"

"Just a moment," said Zenta, frowning. "We can't both go. That would leave the people here completely at the mercy of Ryutaro's men."

"You're right," said Matsuzo. "One of us has to stay. You'd better be the one. Asa has Kongomaru with her, and if you go, he might attack you again."

"But Kongomaru hates the Cat, too," said Zenta.

Hirobei joined the three men by the gate. "What is this about Kongomaru?"

He peered at the tavern keeper, who let the drapery fall over his face again. But he was not quick enough. "What are you doing here, pretending to be a lion dancer?" Hirobei asked the tavern keeper.

The latter had no choice but to repeat what he had told the two ronin.

The merchant was incredulous at first. "Do you mean to say that those peddlers are actually planning an attack on Toshi's house?"

"They have the place surrounded," said the tavern keeper. "And they don't look very friendly."

Hirobei turned to Zenta. "Maybe they're trying to prevent you from going to Asa's rescue."

"It's more than that," insisted the tavern keeper, speaking with a certain relish. "From the looks of their preparation, the peddlers are getting ready to storm this place, seize all the valuables, and rape the women."

Matsuzo was amazed that with Toshi's house under imminent attack, the tavern keeper should venture here himself to deliver the warning. Did he have such a faith in Zenta's ability to fight off the peddlers? Of course he didn't know of Zenta's injury. Or maybe he planned to take advantage of the disorder and join in the looting. At any rate he didn't lack courage.

Nor did Hirobei. He looked more thoughtful than frightened. "I wonder why the peddlers are mounting their attack just now. For more than two years they were satisfied just squeezing money out of the villagers." He turned and looked at the two ronin. "Unless your arrival in the village made a change in the situation."

The merchant was quick, thought Matsuzo. But of course he would be, in any matter involving money. "The Cat wants Asa's inheritence," Matsuzo explained. "Her uncle, Ikken, wants her to marry one of us. That's why the Cat and his peddler confederates have to act quickly."

"I see," said Hirobei slowly. Although he said nothing, he couldn't be pleased by the news that the business he managed for Asa's grandfather might be handed over to one of these two newcomers at the whim of the tea master. But this was not the time for resentment. They were all equally in danger. "If Asa should die at the hands of the Cat, Toshi would inherit the whole fortune," mused the merchant. "That must be why the Cat and Ryutaro's men are mounting their attacks simultaneously. In one stroke they not only get their hands on both Asa and Toshi, they also eliminate other potential suitors for the two women."

Zenta frowned. "That explains why the Cat has ordered Ryutaro to attack this house, but I still don't understand how he can hope to gain possession of Asa's inheritance by assaulting her. The money isn't hers yet."

"We're just wasting time talking!" Matsuzo said impatiently. "Asa is in danger—that much we do know." He turned to the tavern keeper. "You'd better give me some quick lessons in the lion dance."

It was hot under the lion mask. To be sure, Matsuzo was supposed to lift the lion's head up and down in time to the drumming, but he couldn't lift it far for fear of showing his face and the swords strapped to his back. He was also getting tired. Matsuzo was an athletic young man in the best of condition, but hopping and waggling the heavy wooden head brought into action muscles he seldom had occasion to use. He wondered how the tavern keeper had managed to keep up the role. The wiry little man must have had stamina.

The boy who was dancing the rear half of the lion was having trouble keeping up with Matsuzo's long impatient strides. Several times a quick motion from the front half of the lion jerked the cover from the rear half and left the boy exposed. Once the boy had to cry, "Slower, please!" Whereupon Matsuzo stopped suddenly and the boy crashed into him, squeezing the head and the tail of the lion together.

As the lion dance made its way down the main street, the villagers gradually lost their fears and crept out of the houses to watch. Soon the street was crowded with spectators. They cheered and welcomed back the lion dance, something they had missed for several years.

Since graceful, expert dancing was out of the question, the rear half of the lion had evidently decided on low comedy. From the laughter and the comments of the crowd, Matsuzo gathered that the lion was wriggling its rump provocatively.

Several times the dancers were invited to stop and take refreshments. Matsuzo would have pushed on ahead, but the boy whispered, "We must accept, sir. Otherwise the people will become suspicious."

Matsuzo had to drink with his head under the mask. He hoped that the crowd would think that this eccentricity was from his devotion to the role. He was about to refuse the offered food when he suddenly remembered a new friend of his who loved sticky sweets. He took a few of the confections and tucked them into his sleeve.

During a lull in the drumming he heard a bark. For a moment he thought that it was his imagination, because he was just thinking about Kongomaru. Then he heard a louder bark, definitely not his imagination. Raising the lion's head cautiously, Matsuzo saw that down the street a big white dog with black ears was trying to help himself to a tray of confections, while a harassed woman brandished a rice paddle at him.

"It couldn't be Kongomaru!" Matsuzo thought, horrified. But it was, for the torn right ear was unmistakable. Asa was nowhere in sight.

Forgetting his disguise, Matsuzo flung off the lion's head and ran over to the dog. "Kongomaru! Where is Asa?" he demanded.

At the mention of his mistress's name, Kongomaru had the grace to look abashed. He glanced around, as if to say, "Oh yes, my mistress. Now where could I have left her?"

Leaving the tail of the lion to make explanations to the crowd, Matsuzo took a firm grip of Kongomaru and said, "Now take me to Asa. Immediately!"

Kongomaru sniffed wistfully at the sweetmeats in Matsuzo's sleeve. The young ronin said sternly, "No treats for you. Business first!"

As he hurried away with Kongomaru, Matsuzo did not notice a peddler standing at the edge of the crowd looking thoughtfully at them.

In a silent room of the deserted house, Asa huddled close to her lantern, trying to draw a little warmth from its feeble flame. She wondered what was delaying Kiku.

The girl's message had said that she had information about her sister's murder. Perhaps she had seen something the adults had missed. The message didn't specify, for it was very brief and hurriedly scrawled. Asa had been teaching Kiku a little cursive writing, but the writing of the note was crude. Apparently Kiku had been too upset to hold the brush properly.

Asa rubbed her hands and moved her cramped legs, trying to restore circulation. After sitting inactive, she felt her fingers and toes hurting from the cold. She looked uneasily around the bare room, at the corners that her lantern light couldn't quite reach. She wished that Kiku hadn't chosen this particular place for their meeting. The dusty floor, the broken blind, and the torn paper doors all combined to oppress her with a feeling of gloom.

What lay most heavily on Asa's mind was the thought that a girl had been murdered in this very room. Picking up her lantern, Asa rose and examined one of the windows. She could still see a few strips of paper that had been used to seal the windows. But in spite of the efforts to keep away the evil spirits, the victim had complained of headaches and dizziness. Nor had the precautions prevented her murder.

Asa suddenly looked down at her feet. Could she be standing on the very spot where the girl's body had been found? The wooden floor, covered with dust, showed no stains, but there was a dark patch on the wall in front of her. It could have been caused by the damp, of course. Asa turned her eyes away hastily.

It had been foolish of her to come, Asa now admitted. Her mother would never have allowed her to come if she had known. She should have sent word to Kiku to arrange a meeting at a safer place in broad daylight. Her reason for coming had been a desire to show Uncle Ikken—and the two young samurai—that she was braver than they had thought. If she could obtain some information on the murders, how impressed they would be!

But now her earlier courage and confidence had almost drained away during the long and cold wait. Asa decided that if Kiku didn't appear soon, she would leave. People would be paying New Year's calls at her home, and her mother needed her to help entertain the guests.

She was glad that she had Kongomaru's company at least. Suddenly she felt an urge to put her arms around his neck and feel his warm breath on her cheek. He was sitting outside on the veranda, as a well-behaved dog should, but since the house had long been abandoned, what was to stop her from having him in?

Asa rose, went to the door, and pushed it open a little. "Come here, Kongomaru," she called.

Kongomaru didn't answer. Puzzled, she looked out and saw that the veranda was empty. Perhaps he was in the small garden, discovering an old buried bone. "Kongomaru!" she called again, more loudly.

Still the dog didn't answer. Uncle Hirobei was right. Kongomaru was easily tempted away by strangers offering treats. Lately he had been going off more and more often, and worst of all he seemed to have become friendly with the medicine peddlers.

Just as she was about to open the door wider and step out, she heard a faint sound behind her. Someone was walking softly in the back room.

The house was a small one, with two main rooms separated by a sliding door. Asa was in the larger room, which faced the front garden, and the footsteps were coming from the smaller room, which led to the kitchen and the back door.

Of course. The steps were being made by Kiku. The girl was coming stealthily because she didn't want the neighbors to know of their meeting.

The paper of the door separating the two rooms was torn, and through the gaps Asa thought she saw a dark shape moving in the other room. "Kiku, is that you?" she asked.

For a moment the soft footsteps stopped. Then Asa heard a sound that made her heart lurch with fear. It was a thin, mewing sound. The Cat. She was alone in the house with the Cat.

Fear constricted her throat, so that she couldn't even scream. She could only stare at the door to the back room as it slowly slid open.

A dark figure filled the doorway. It looked totally black except for its eyes, which reflected tiny sparks of light from the lantern. Almost lazily the Cat passed through the door and began approaching her.

Asa tried to back away, but she had difficulty making her legs obey her. She could only stumble back. The Cat moved forward, taking its time and making mewing noises. She was in a nightmare, and everything swam slowly in a thick liquid. The mewing, nightmarish voice was saying something intelligible: "You can't escape me, Asa."

Suddenly her foot struck the lantern and knocked it over. The room was plunged into darkness. The mewing noise was closer, and it came in sharp bursts. Asa realized that it was the Cat laughing. She retreated until her back was against the door to the veranda. With her hands behind her she fumbled frantically until she felt the door slide open.

It was then that she heard footsteps behind her as well. She fainted.

Asa was roused by the sound of furious barking. She opened her eyes to find herself lying on the veranda, while inside the room Kongomaru was engaged in a furious struggle with the Cat. There was a hiss and a sword flashed out.

Asa screamed. Then steel clashed against steel, and there was a burst of sparks.

"Stay back, Kongomaru, but keep a watch on him," said a voice—a normal human voice.

Almost crying with relief, Asa recognized the newcomer as Matsuzo. It had been his footsteps she had just heard. The young ronin stood motionless, his face rigid with concentration. Only his sword moved very slightly, responding to the movements of his adversary.

Asa forced herself to look at the Cat. Now that the door to the outside was open, she had enough reflected light from the snow to see him more clearly. He was dressed all in black, and his face was completely covered except for his eyes. He gave such an impression of power and ruthlessness that he looked almost superhuman. And yet he had not emerged unscathed from the struggle with Kongomaru. A trickle of blood was visible on the back of his right hand, which was partly thrust into the front of his kimono. He held his sword with his left hand alone.

Asa wondered why Matsuzo did not immediately attack. The advantages seemed to be on his side, for he had Kongomaru's help and the Cat could use only one hand. She did not know what Matsuzo knew, that some fighters—Zenta was one—could use a sword better with one hand than most men could with both hands.

Suddenly the Cat moved. His right hand whipped out and something whistled in the air. Matsuzo quickly stepped back as Asa screamed. Kongomaru sprang, but was just a fraction of a second too late. There was a rip, and then the black figure jumped back and bounded away into the darkness.

Asa had just enough presence of mind to call Kongomaru back. She would rather let the Cat escape than risk pitting Kongomaru against a killer with a sword. It took several calls before the dog obeyed, for he clearly harbored a violent hatred of the Cat.

She turned to Matsuzo and saw with concern that he was dabbing at his throat with a paper tissue. "Are you wounded?" she asked.

"No, it's just a scratch," said Matsuzo, looking puzzled.

Asa looked at the scratch and saw that it was long but fortunately not deep. "It's strange, but I didn't see him or his sword anywhere near you," she said. "Of course I don't have a trained eye, and everything happened very quickly."

"You weren't mistaken," said Matsuzo. "His sword didn't touch me. In fact we were far apart after our initial clash. The funny thing is that this is exactly what happened to Zenta, too. Last night, just before we first met you, Zenta was trying to catch the Cat by surprise. He also received a scratch on his throat, and he claimed that he was nowhere near the Cat. Just now, did you see whether the Cat had some other kind of weapon? One that shot a projectile?"

"No . . . I didn't see anything," said Asa. She began to shake as the reaction from her recent experiences set in. "The village people claim that the Cat can lengthen his arm and kill over a long distance. That was how Kiku's sister was murdered this morning."

"I don't believe any of that nonsense," said Matsuzo firmly. He turned to Kongomaru and patted him. "That was good work, Kongomaru. I'm not sure I would have been a match for the Cat without your help."

He bent down and removed something from Kongomaru's jaws. "What do you have here? Another scrap from the enemy?"

Asa looked at the scrap of black cloth from Kongomaru's mouth. The young ronin examined it carefully and then held it to his nose. "Yes, this piece of cloth has the same smell that the last one did, only this time the smell is stronger because the scrap is much bigger." Suddenly he went completely still.

"What is it?" cried Asa.

"I think I recognize the smell now," Matsuzo replied.

11

After Matsuzo left, Zenta asked Hirobei to break the news of the siege to Toshi and the servants. The household staff might panic and do something rash when they heard that cutthroats were surrounding their house and planning an attack. It would be fatal if they rushed out from a back entrance and tried to escape. Since Hirobei acted almost like the head of the house, the staff would be less alarmed if the news came from him.

Toshi took the news well. Her first reaction was anxiety for Asa, but when she heard that Matsuzo had gone to her daughter's rescue, she was somewhat reassured and went to calm the maidservants. They turned out to need less calming than the male staff. The women were outraged at the idea of being attacked on New Year's Day, a day reserved for feasting and rejoicing. It was the one occasion when they could rest from their hard work and enjoy themselves. More angry than frightened, the women immediately set about finding weapons to defend themselves. They vowed they would not be easy victims.

On the other hand the menservants looked fearful, especially the gatekeeper. The tavern keeper tried to get some spirit into them by jeering at them, but he had little success.

"Do you think any of the staff would desert to the enemy?" Zenta asked Hirobei. "Perhaps we should lock up the untrustworthy ones before they do any harm."

"I know they look pretty useless, but they aren't treacherous," said Hirobei quickly. "I can vouch for them myself."

Zenta next took stock of the weapons. Toshi had brought out all the weapons that used to belong to her husband—some very fine swords and a few spears. The question was, who would be able to use them?

"I'll try one of these," said the tavern keeper, picking up a spear and waving it. "It looks easier than a sword. All you have to do is hold the blunt end and poke with the sharp end."

Zenta stepped back out of range. "Well, there's a little more to it than that, but I haven't time to go into it now. Just remember: poke at the enemy, not at one of us."

To Hirobei he said, "The peddlers don't know that Matsuzo has left. After that attempted ambush, they must know that he is good. They won't be in a hurry to attack." Zenta had no way of knowing that Matsuzo had been seen in the village street by one of the peddlers.

Hirobei picked up one of the swords and tried it for

balance. Zenta could see that he knew how to handle the weapon. The man interested him more and more. "How did you happen to learn swordsmanship?" he asked the merchant.

Hirobei smiled grimly. "I have to travel a great deal on business, often with large sums of money. Since the roads aren't very safe these days, I decided that I needed a few lessons on how to discourage unwelcome traveling companions."

Toshi approached with a suggestion. "Shall I light the fire and heat some sake? It might put the men into better spirits."

"Fire!" exclaimed Zenta, cursing himself for overlooking this obvious danger. "Put out all the fires at once! We must also guard against fire arrows from the enemy. Get all the vessels you have in the house and fill them with water from the well. We should have some soaking wet quilts as well for smothering out flames."

Entering the kitchen to make sure of the fires, he found the cook and her assistants busily sharpening a number of very wicked-looking knives. One of the women gave him a ferocious grin. "Tonight our knives will be cutting something other than food."

Plenty of fight here, thought Zenta. Just as he was stepping down into the back courtyard, he heard a cry, followed by a crash. One of the menservants got up painfully and rubbed his back. "Somebody spilled water here and it froze into ice!"

That gave Zenta an idea. There was a great deal of snow around the house, and by packing it down with their feet and pouring a little water, they could make the ground slippery and cause the downfall of the unwary enemy. He immediately gave orders to create several icy patches at the base of the walls where assailants scaling the walls would be likely to land.

"Since I can't be everywhere at once," he said thoughtfully, "it would be helpful if we could set up something that would make a noise when the enemy lands. It would act as an alarm for me."

Toshi overheard him. "We have plenty of pots, pans, and dishes," she said. "We could place stacks of them around, so that anyone brushing against them would send them toppling with a clatter."

"Excellent!" said Zenta, laughing. He was glad to see her enter enthusiastically into his plans for the defense. She seemed to have overcome her antagonism toward the samurai class, or at least toward him. If she felt any nervousness about the imminent attack, she hid it well. Her example gave courage to her staff, and they jumped to obey Zenta's orders.

Walking around the house to inspect the defense, Zenta saw the tavern keeper giving lessons on using the spear to the quaking gatekeeper. Once a spear butt went through a papered window, and the two men looked around guiltily to see if Toshi had noticed. As he watched the wild swings of the spears, Zenta hoped that the two men would inflict more damage on the enemy than on themselves. At least it was better than having the gatekeeper sit worrying about the dangers and making everyone else nervous as well. On the whole the morale of the staff was as good as could be expected. They were all tense, but they were pretty much in control of their fear.

While Zenta was discussing how to post their men with Hirobei, there was a knocking on the gate. The gatekeeper went to look through the peephole and came back trembling. "It's Ryutaro, sir," he told Zenta. "He wants to talk to you."

"That means he knows we are expecting him," said Zenta. "Did he guess that the lion dancers came to give warning?"

It was already dark, and through the peephole of the heavy gate Zenta could see that the peddlers had set up a number of tripods with iron baskets holding flaming logs. The illumination provided by the flames showed Ryutaro standing empty-handed in front of the gate.

"I have something private to say, and I can't shout it through the gate," said the leader of the peddlers. "Can you come out?"

"You must take me for a fool if you think I'm going to do that," said Zenta.

Ryutaro opened his arms wide. "Look: I'm not armed. You'll be safe."

Zenta laughed. "You can't be serious. What's to prevent you from having archers trained on me?"

"Your position is hopeless!" said Ryutaro impatiently. "We know that you are the only swordsman in there. Your friend has been killed by the Cat."

It was a stunning blow. For a moment Zenta was too numb to feel anything. When he did, it was mainly guilt. He was the one who had brought Matsuzo into this. But guilt, regret, grief, they would have to wait. There were desperate matters to attend to first.

Zenta took a deep breath and forced himself into calmness. He had to think. Why was Ryutaro so anxious to parley? He was stamping his feet, perhaps from impatience rather than cold. The peddler *was* anxious, there was no doubt about that. Could he be lying about Matsuzo's death?

"Where is the Cat?" demanded Zenta. "Why isn't he here to take part in the siege?"

"The Cat wanted the girl, Asa," replied Ryutaro. "In fact that was how your friend was killed. He was trying to protect the girl from the Cat."

"Why wasn't Kongomaru guarding his mistress?" asked Zenta. "He hates the Cat violently."

There was a slight pause. Then Ryutaro said, "It's easy to tempt the dog with treats. We got him away so that the Cat could attack the girl without interference."

Ryutaro's hesitation was not lost on Zenta. He felt a stirring of hope. "Produce Kongomaru, then. I'll be convinced when I see the dog here with you."

Suddenly there was a crash of pots and pans, followed by bloodcurdling yells. Zenta turned and ran to the back of the house. "Treacherous devil!" he thought angrily. "Trying to hold my attention while one of his men is scaling the walls!"

He found that one of Ryutaro's men had used a grappling hook to climb over the back wall, only to fall flat on his back on a patch of ice. A pack of women, yelling and screaming, had promptly rushed up to attack him with their knives. One of them turned to Zenta and said, "No need to trouble yourself here, sir. We'll take care of him."

Zenta winced and turned away. He had taken part in countless fights, but illogically, the thought of being stabbed to death by kitchen knives sickened him.

He heard several sharp clicks. Glistening on the top of the wall were more grappling hooks. The tavern keeper rushed over, eagerly trailing his spear. He promptly slipped on a patch of ice and fell. As he struggled to get up, one of the peddlers dropped down from the wall and landed on top of him. The gatekeeper ran up with his spear to help his teacher, the tavern keeper. For a while the three men and the two spears became a knot of arms, legs, and spear butts. Every now and then one of the three would slip and fall, dragging the other two down with him.

Zenta didn't wait to see the outcome of the complicated struggle, for he had heard the distant crash of crockery, which meant that more assailants had climbed the walls. Immediately behind him there were thuds as two more peddlers dropped down from the top of the wall. The men managed to hit places that were not icy, and they landed well, with swords ready in their hands.

In a single flowing motion Zenta ducked under one attacker, drew his sword with his left hand, slashed at the second man, and whirled around to cut down the first man.

Hirobei arrived in time to see the two men fall. "You certainly don't waste time or energy," he said. "As a practical merchant, I approve of this economy."

Zenta's swordsmanship had often been admired for

its power and speed, but this was the first time a merchant had praised him for economy. He felt absurdly pleased by the compliment. "I don't have any time or energy to waste," he said, laughing. "How is the kitchen staff doing in your section? I heard a crash of utensils."

"We're doing well enough," said Hirobei carelessly. "I killed one man as he climbed over the wall, and the women took care of the other."

Zenta looked at Hirobei with respect. His sleeves expertly tied back to reveal unexpectedly muscular arms, the well-fed merchant with the chubby face was proving to be an efficient ally. Their situation was beginning to look less hopeless. Zenta thought that there was a chance they might win what he mentally called the Battle of the Pots and Pans. Ryutaro had already lost six men, not counting the three Matsuzo had killed earlier. The peddlers could not afford this rate of loss for long.

The thought of Matsuzo, however, brought back Zenta's anxiety over his young friend. What had really happened between Matsuzo and the Cat?

Zenta pushed aside these speculations. He couldn't afford to indulge in mental anguish over Matsuzo's fate, for he had to concentrate on the present dangers. Ryutaro's men had apparently given up their attempts to scale the walls. What would they try next? An attempt to set the house on fire was a possibility, but the defenders were fairly well prepared for that, unless a fire arrow were to land out of reach on the roof.

The peddlers might try to make a breach in the wall. Most of the walls of the village houses were of flimsy materials, bamboo sticks lashed with twine or even bundles of sedge grass tied together. The walls surrounding Toshi's house, however, were more solidly built. Her late husband might have turned merchant, but he had the walls built with a warrior's eye to defense.

While he was inspecting for possible weaknesses Zenta's eye was caught by a grappling hook still left attached to the slate tiles on top of the wall. It was the size of a human hand, and it gave the impression of someone clinging to the other side of the wall. In the flickering light from the flaming logs, the sharp steel prongs of the grappling hook glittered and reminded Zenta of something: they looked like the talons of a beast.

So that was it, thought Zenta. He was beginning to see how the Cat was able to attack over a distance.

His thoughts were interrupted by the tavern keeper, who limped up with a satisfied smirk on his face. "We managed to kill that peddler for you, sir. That's one less to worry about."

"Are you getting the feel of the spear pretty well?" asked Zenta.

"Well, some of the papered windows in this house will never be the same again," admitted the tavern keeper. "But we'll do better with the next man. Of course he'll have to slip and fall on his back."

Once more there was a pounding on the front gate. Determined not to be tricked again, Zenta gave orders for extra vigilance while he went to investigate.

It was Ryutaro at the gate again, and the urgency in his voice was apparent. "You can't last much longer," the peddler called. "You have only a fat merchant and some frightened servants to help you."

"The fat merchant and the frightened servants have already killed six of your men," said Zenta. "Why don't you send a few more over the walls? With so little action here, we're getting rather bored."

He could hear a fierce argument on the other side of the gate. Ryutaro was trying to reassure his men, who were clearly growing desperate. Several times Zenta heard the Cat mentioned, and he now realized why Ryutaro wanted his immediate surrender. Perhaps the Cat suspected that Ryutaro had attempted to ally himself with Zenta. Since the peddlers were so slow in overcoming the people in the house, the Cat might think that they were not trying very hard.

"We're comfortable here, and we can hold out indefinitely," taunted Zenta. "But your people seem to be getting desperate. What's the matter? Has the Cat been threatening you?"

The sudden silence on the other side of the gate told him that he had struck a sensitive spot. Finally Ryutaro said, "All right, I admit that I'm afraid of the Cat, and I'm afraid of what he will do when he finds out that I haven't broken down your resistance. I beg you, open the gate and join forces with me. We'll fight the Cat together. You can name your conditions."

Ryutaro was desperate, there was no doubt about that. But how far could he be trusted? Zenta couldn't be sure that if he opened the gate and went out, the peddlers wouldn't attack him immediately. "You'll have to face the Cat's displeasure by yourself," he told Ryutaro. "I'm staying here."

"You've had your chance, and now we're going to batter down your gates!" shouted Ryutaro.

"We'll be ready for you," replied Zenta.

Good materials had gone into the construction of the front gate. Zenta knew that only heavy battering would break it down, and a good strong pole would not be easy to find. He had time to make his preparations.

The women knife wielders had lost some of their earlier confidence. Seeing that their enthusiasm had been cooled by Ryutaro's threat to break down the gate, Zenta decided not to give them time to become thoroughly frightened.

"Get as much snow here as you can and pack it down," he told the women. "We want to prepare a long, slippery path beginning about three paces from the gate."

To the gatekeeper, he said, "Slip back the bar of the gate until it will open at the slightest pressure. Do it quietly so that the people on the other side won't know."

"You w-want the g-gate to op-open easily?" stammered the gatekeeper.

"I want them to come rushing in and slip on the ice," explained Zenta patiently. "And we need the gate intact because we'll have to close it again afterward."

The tavern keeper hurried up eagerly. "Shall I spear all the men who slip and fall?"

Zenta took the tavern keeper's spear and reversed its direction. "Remember: blunt end toward our side, sharp end toward the enemy."

He turned to Hirobei. "You'll see to it, won't you, that those who are on the ground don't get up again?"

Hirobei nodded calmly. "What about the rest of the peddlers who will swarm in after the gate is opened? That will be your job, I suppose?"

"Yes, that will be my job," said Zenta. He was not happy about the condition of his right hand, but there was no point in alarming the others.

The snow, sprinkled with a little water, created a long treacherous stretch in front of the gate. The constant stamping of many feet had already polished most of the snow into ice. Having done all they could, the defenders now waited for the assault. And they did not have long to wait.

They heard some grunts and then a chorus of voices saying, "All together now: let's go!"

There was a rush of feet, followed by a bang, and the gate burst wide open.

The ramming party had expected to use all their force on the stoutly built gate. When it flew open with almost no resistance, the men came hurtling through, slid across the icy stretch out of control, and fell crashing down. Every single man of the ramming party lay stunned.

The tavern keeper and the kitchen women ran up to attack the fallen men, but Zenta didn't stop to look at them. He was fully occupied with the men who tried to follow the first party through the open gate.

Most swordsmen used both hands to wield the longer of the two samurai swords and reserved the shorter one for committing hara-kiri. A few, however, developed the technique of using both swords, one in each hand. Zenta belonged to this small group, and he was glad that he had spent years perfecting this technique. Still unable to use his right hand properly, he was able to use his left hand independently. Little by little, he drove the attackers back.

If the defenders were to close the gate again, they would need the area immediately in front of it cleared of attackers. To do that Zenta would have to venture some distance out of the gate. It was risky, for he could be easily surrounded by the enemy and cut off. But the gate had to be closed, and soon. The defenders were getting tired and needed a rest from fighting.

As Zenta began his slashing attack to drive the besiegers back from the gate, he saw to his surprise that Hirobei was fighting beside him. The merchant seemed to have a good grasp of the situation and realized that Zenta needed to protect his back. The besiegers were unprepared for the attack, for they had not expected that the defenders would actually venture out and take the offensive.

The immediate area around the gate was now cleared of the enemy. Zenta ran back quickly, and he was already inside the gate before he realized that Hirobei was not with him. He looked back and saw that the merchant was still standing some distance outside. He seemed to be clutching his ribs. Some of the peddlers were cautiously advancing again.

"Shall I close the gate, sir?" asked the nervous gate-keeper.

"No, wait!" ordered Zenta.

He rushed out of the gate and ran to Hirobei, who was swaying. "I'll . . . be . . . all right. . . . " the merchant gasped.

Then the enemy was upon them. They seemed to gather courage from the fact that Zenta would be fighting alone.

Above the cries and gasps of the combatants, Zenta suddenly heard the noise of a great number of people approaching.

"If those are reinforcements for the peddlers, then we're lost," he thought in despair.

12

Matsuzo was in a frantic hurry to go back to Toshi's house and see how the siege was going, but Asa was shivering violently from shock and cold, and he knew he had to bring her immediately to a warm shelter. The nearby houses looked dark and deserted. The noise of his fight and the mewing of the Cat had probably driven the neighborhood people back into their homes. Desperately he looked around for a place of safety for Asa.

Then he remembered Jiro, the carpenter. Since Asa had come to meet Kiku, the carpenter's daughter, Jiro's house could not be far off.

"Asa," he said to the girl, "where is Jiro's house? If you tell me where it is, I'll take you there."

Asa was shaking so much that she had difficulty speaking. She finally pointed in the direction of the house.

Matsuzo picked her up and carried her, with Kongomaru following protectively behind.

At Jiro's gate Matsuzo's calls produced no response. He was not surprised. After a while he could hear a shutter being stealthily pushed open. Finally Kongomaru gave a few short, impatient barks.

Matsuzo heard some voices. "What did I tell you?" said a man's voice. "That wasn't the Cat. That was Kongomaru, the young lady's dog."

A woman's voice said, "All right, we can let them in."

The gate opened to reveal a middle-aged man carrying a lantern. Peeking from behind him was a woman, obviously his wife. When she saw Matsuzo carrying Asa, she screamed and rushed forward. "Oh, no, not another murder!"

"Asa isn't hurt, but she has had a bad shock and is nearly frozen," replied Matsuzo. "Can we put her to bed here and get her warm?"

That set the household bustling. While Jiro fanned up the flames of a charcoal brazier, his wife went off to prepare hot soup. Soon a girl appeared, and Matsuzo learned that she was Kiku, the younger sister of the carpenter's murdered daughter.

"Did you write a message to Asa asking her to meet you in the abandoned house?" he asked the girl.

Kiku had been rubbing her eyes sleepily, but at Matsuzo's question her eyes opened wide. "Message? I didn't write any message."

Matsuzo nodded. Kiku's answer confirmed his suspicion that it had been a spurious message sent by the Cat to lure Asa into a trap.

Leaving Asa to the care of Kiku and her mother, Matsuzo turned to Jiro and told him how Asa had come to be in the empty house.

When the carpenter at first showed little reaction to the horrifying account, Matsuzo realized he must still be numb with grief. The man had lost his older daughter only that morning.

But at Matsuzo's mention of the fight with the Cat, some animation and color came into Jiro's face. He got up and called to his wife. "Did you hear that? This young gentleman has seen the Cat in person and has actually fought with him!"

The carpenter's wife came and stared at Matsuzo with awe. "And you're still alive to tell the story?"

"I'm not sure that I'd be alive if Kongomaru hadn't attacked the Cat first," Matsuzo admitted. "He even managed to draw blood!"

Kongomaru was sitting outside on the veranda. At the mention of his name he gave a short bark of acknowledgment. Matsuzo thought he detected a note in the bark hinting that some reward in the form of food would not be refused.

Once it became clear that the Cat was not a supernatural demon but a mere human being, there was a visible change in Jiro and his wife. Grief over their daughter's death was replaced by anger. "I'll call the neighbors," the carpenter said. "They should know about this."

In a short time there was a crowd of excited villagers

in the main room of the carpenter's house. Their resentment mounted as they heard Matsuzo explain how the peddlers worked together with the Cat and used the charcoal brazier in the sealed room to induce faintness.

"That exorcist!" cried one man. "Why, I watched him grow up. I always knew he would turn out badly!"

They began to compare stories on the strange behavior of the exorcist. Matsuzo had to interrupt and bring their attention back to Ryutaro and the Cat. He needed the help of these villagers. Surely the attack on Toshi's house must have reached a critical stage by now, and Zenta would be sorely pressed.

Now that some of the supernatural elements had been explained, the villagers began to lose their fear. Matsuzo had the satisfaction of seeing the feeling in the room grow bold and even reckless.

"I have some tools that would make good weapons," declared the carpenter. "With this samurai as our leader, we can attack these murderers and avenge our daughters!"

Several farmers offered to get hoes and sickles to use as weapons. The womenfolk, no less bold than the men, declared themselves ready to use their kitchen knives.

Matsuzo was impatient to move quickly. With Zenta the only fighting man at Toshi's house, it was hard to see how he could hold out against Ryutaro's attack. The young ronin realized, however, that he had to organize the villagers first. Unlike Zenta, Matsuzo had had no experience commanding troops, but he did know that if he led a confused rabble against Ryutaro's men, he would be bringing them straight to their deaths. He tried to recall what he had learned from Zenta. The first thing was to find some lieutenants, since he couldn't give orders directly to so many men at once.

"How many of you have ever served in a war before?" he asked.

Two of the farmers had served as foot soldiers. It was at that time common for farmers to become soldiers and then revert back to being farmers when they felt the land needed them. The class distinction between warriors and farmers had not become completely rigid.

Matsuzo instructed the two men to organize their fellow farmers into a compact group that would follow their orders. He himself would lead the village craftsmen with their miscellaneous weapons. He looked over the men under his command: their equipment certainly didn't lack variety. Jiro was the best armed, with his ax and his chisel. The mason and the barrel maker both had mallets that could dent a few skulls, and the iron-smith had a long-handled anvil hammer capable of striking a hard blow. The strangest weapon belonged to the brewer: a long paddle used for stirring sake in vats.

Matsuzo's hardest task was to persuade Jiro's wife and several women armed with knives to stay behind and guard Asa. They all wanted to join the avenging party, but he eventually persuaded them that Asa needed more protection than just Kongomaru. Before setting out he reminded the women to feed Kongomaru. With a full stomach the dog would be less likely to stray.

The young ronin decided to lead the villagers against the peddlers before their exuberance had time to fade. As they rushed down the village street toward Asa's house, their numbers were increased by others who had heard the news and hastened to join them. Matsuzo smiled a little at the sight of his irregular troops. Well, the troops under Zenta's command were just as irregular. At the thought of the besieged Matsuzo's sense of urgency returned and he quickened his steps.

Well before they reached Asa's house they were able to hear the sounds of fierce fighting. For a terrible moment Matsuzo thought that the peddlers had succeeded in breaking down the defense and were already killing, pillaging, and raping. Then he saw that the action was taking place outside the walls. To his immense relief he saw that Zenta was fighting in the midst of the peddlers and was holding his own.

"Come on!" Matsuzo called to his men. "If we don't hurry, my friend will finish the fight by himself!"

The villagers behind Matsuzo didn't need a second urging. Scenting victory the band rushed down on the peddlers with bloodthirsty yells. In the lead were Matsuzo with sword in hand and the two veteran farmers waving their spears. To the peddlers the yelling horde must have looked like an advancing army. The peddlers broke and began to retreat.

The collapse of their enemy did not satisfy the villagers: they attacked with even greater fury. Some of the tripods and their flaming baskets were toppled during the melee. In the mounting darkness and confusion Matsuzo found the grunts and groans around him more animal-like than human. He hunted for an opponent worthy of his sword. Where was Ryutaro?

Finally, leaving the villagers to chase down the stragglers, Matsuzo looked around for Zenta. He found his friend helping up a man who appeared to be wounded. As Matsuzo went to Zenta's aid the light from a nearby torch fell on the wounded man's face. Matsuzo started with surprise. It was Hirobei, a man he had expected to find cowering with fear inside the house. It looked as if he had misjudged the merchant.

Hirobei must have noticed Matsuzo's surprise. He smiled and said, "After this, I'm going back to my account books."

As the two ronin helped Hirobei up the steps to the house, Toshi ran to them, almost stumbling in her haste. "Is he badly hurt?" she cried.

Up to then Matsuzo had only seen Toshi's casual treatment of Hirobei. Now it seemed that her usual manner toward her father's business manager may have hidden her real feelings. When Hirobei's wound was found to be a long but shallow slash across the ribs, however, she reverted to her old manner. "Next time, stay out of trouble and stop trying to pretend that you're a samurai," she said tartly.

After she had bandaged Hirobei and made him comfortable, Toshi left to inspect the damage to the house. Zenta sat down and regarded the merchant thoughtfully. "The business trip you made this morning, was it connected with Toshi?"

Hirobei frowned and for a moment looked as if he wouldn't answer. Then he said reluctantly, "I suppose you are bound to know sooner or later. The fact is, I went to visit Toshi's father and asked him if I could marry her. Naturally, I told him that I wouldn't want any of his money."

"Did Toshi know about your intention?" asked Zenta.

"She didn't say so, but I think she suspected," said Hirobei. "We've liked each other for many years, long before she married the tea master's brother."

This tale of selfless love wasn't completely convincing to Matsuzo, and he could tell that Zenta was also somewhat skeptical. "You say that you wouldn't want any money from Toshi's father," said Zenta, "but if Asa should die and the money went to Toshi, you wouldn't refuse it, would you?"

Hirobei raised his eyebrows. "What do you think? There have been moments, especially during the last few days, when I really thought Asa might not have long to live. That's why I had to hurry. If I tried to marry Toshi after Asa's death, I would look like a fortune hunter."

Calculating, thought Matsuzo disgustedly. And yet he had to admit that Hirobei was at least frank.

"Toshi herself had no desire to marry into the samurai class," said Hirobei. For the first time he showed a trace of anger. "It was her father who had insisted on the match with the tea master's brother. After he made his money, he became a social climber and wanted to be connected by marriage to an old samurai family. Toshi's husband became the official head of the business, but I was the one who did all the real work."

"Why doesn't Toshi's father live here with his daughter?" asked Zenta. "Since he adopted his son-in-law, that would have been the normal thing to do."

Hirobei's smile was cynical. "His son-in-law made him nervous. The old man was proud of his connection with Ikken's family, but he didn't enjoy living under the critical eye of an ex-samurai. He was always finding business reasons for living away from his daughter and her husband. Toshi hates the way her father grovels to her in-laws."

"You don't show any tendency to grovel," said Zenta, smiling.

Matsuzo was surprised to see that Zenta really seemed to have developed a liking for the merchant. They must have worked well together during the siege. But Hirobei didn't respond to Zenta's smile. "I suppose one of you will now marry Asa," he said. "Her grandfather will be very pleased."

"I have no intention of marrying Asa," said Zenta.

"Nor I," added Matsuzo quickly.

"That's what you say," said Hirobei. "But can I believe you?"

"It doesn't matter whether you believe us or not!" snapped Matsuzo.

Zenta stood up. "You're tired, and your wound must be uncomfortable. We'll leave you to rest."

"Impertinent rascal," muttered Matsuzo as he followed Zenta out of the room.

In the front courtyard the two ronin found an impromptu victory party in progress. Slightly hysterical with relief at their narrow escape, Toshi's staff had taken it upon themselves to bring out all their boxes of New Year's food and serve it to the victors. They had also rolled out whole kegs of sake. The staff and the villagers alike were helping themselves liberally to the wine. Without bothering to heat it first and impatient with the small china wine cups, the villagers poured the sake directly into rice bowls. These they found conveniently strewn about the ground near the base of the walls. Gusts of laughter burst out here and there as the maidservants explained the reason for the piles of crockery.

Matsuzo accepted a brimming rice bowl handed to him unsteadily by a tipsy maid. Some of the wine spilled, and the rest he drank off almost in one gulp, for he was thirsty from his strenuous work.

As a villager wove his way back to the sake keg, Zenta stopped him. "Can you tell me what happened to the rest of the peddlers outside?"

The man beamed with triumph and drink. "We're chasing down the last of the peddlers," he told the ronin. "The curse of the Vampire Cat is over!"

Matsuzo thought the villagers' celebration was premature. His recent encounter with the Cat had given him the impression that his opponent was a dangerous and powerful fighter, not someone who could be chased down by a pack of peasants.

But there was no damping the enthusiasm of the crowd. Released from three years of fear and oppression, the villagers threw themselves into a wild celebration. Matsuzo saw that the lion dance had started in the courtyard, accompanied by a frenzied drumbeat. More and more people jostled with each other to join the dance, and soon there were so many participants that the rear of the lion had become a wiggling snake.

In another corner of the courtyard the tavern keeper was describing the siege to an admiring audience. "Listening to him, you'd think he had organized the defense all by himself," Matsuzo said to Zenta. "I suspect he was hiding in a cupboard behind a pile of bedding the whole time."

"You're wrong," said Zenta. "He actually did kill one of the peddlers with his spear, just as he said. You shouldn't underestimate these villagers. Look at the men you led. When you all charged down on the house, I thought it was the army of some neighboring warlord!"

"They were pretty frightening," Matsuzo agreed. "When I told them how the exorcist induced fainting fits by using the special charcoal, the villagers became furious. By the way, what happened to the exorcist? Was he killed?"

The two ronin looked over the dead bodies near the front gate, but they didn't find the exorcist. Eventually they asked a villager, and the man replied that the exorcist had been one of the first to run off. "He's probably in the next province by now," said the villager, grinning. "He isn't very bright, but he's smart enough to know that things won't be healthy for him around here."

Every now and then Matsuzo heard distant cries as the villagers found another peddler and attacked him with their rustic weapons. The young ronin was disturbed by their bloodlust, but he knew they couldn't be denied their vengeance. The peddlers, after all, deserved little pity.

Finally one pitiful moan proved too much for Matsuzo. He went over and pushed into a circle of men who were attacking someone on the ground. Raising his sword, he was just about to dispatch the man cleanly when Zenta held his arm. "Wait. The man is trying to say something."

The man was dying, and his words came in gasps.

All his remaining strength was concentrated on what he had to say. "You . . . hunted us . . . when we were . . . defeated. . . . Your women robbed . . . the dead. . . . You deserved what the Cat . . . " He choked and lay still.

The villagers fell silent and stood with heads bent. After a while they shuffled away and joined their friends in the torchlit courtyard, where the celebration continued unabated.

"Do you think the man was talking about the battle that took place here a few years ago?" Matsuzo asked his companion.

Zenta nodded. "I think the Cat and some of the peddlers must be among the defeated who survived the battle. Perhaps the Vampire Cat was their way of getting revenge on the village."

"Hunting down the defeated and looting the dead!" said Matsuzo indignantly. "I can almost understand the motives of the Cat."

"Nothing can excuse the murders," said Zenta curtly.

Matsuzo suddenly remembered that Asa was still with the carpenter's family. "Now that the fighting has died down here, it's safe to bring Asa back again," he said.

"Asa is already back," said Toshi, overhearing them. "Jiro couldn't wait to tell his wife about the victory. She came to join the celebration and brought Asa with her."

Toshi's face was flushed and her hair had fallen loose, making her look like a young girl in the torchlight. For the first time Matsuzo realized that she was beautiful. Perhaps Hirobei's interest in her was not entirely mercenary after all.

At Toshi's invitation, the two ronin returned to the

house for refreshments. Matsuzo went eagerly, for he was ravenous. Zenta, too, would want to eat before any further action, which both men knew would be necessary, in spite of the villagers' optimism. As long as the enemy leaders were still at large, the danger was not ended.

"So you were in time to rescue Asa after all," Zenta said as they removed their footgear and stepped up into the house. "Tell me about your fight with the Cat. What did you think of his swordsmanship?"

"He was good," said Matsuzo without hesitation. "After his right hand had been hurt by Kongomaru, he held his sword with his left hand alone. I could tell that he was accustomed to fighting one-handed."

He stopped for a moment and then said, "You know, the curious thing is that in some ways he reminded me of you. Not only in the technique of the sword, but also in build and the way he moved."

Zenta was sitting down on the floor examining the blade of his sword. At Matsuzo's last words he looked up sharply. After staring for some seconds he dropped his eyes and went back to his sword. "Was his right hand badly hurt?" he asked.

Matsuzo had the impression that Zenta had intended to say something different. But he answered the question. "His hand was bleeding, but he could still use it."

He suddenly remembered the Cat whipping something out with his right hand. "I think he had a weapon that shot a projectile of some sort. It nearly got me in the neck, but I ducked in time."

Zenta relaxed. "I know what the weapon is. It's a

grappling hook. The Cat swings it out at the end of a rope."

Matsuzo pictured the steel prongs at the end of a grappling hook and couldn't suppress a shudder. Using the hook was a vicious idea, the product of a sadistic mind. "The Cat is a strong swordsman, I'm positive of it," he said. "He doesn't need to use a hook to kill his victims."

"No, he must derive some sort of enjoyment from tearing out the throat of his victim," said Zenta.

"How did he swing the hook without being seen?" asked Matsuzo. "I should have caught a flash of the metal hook as it—" He stopped, for he saw the answer himself. "I see. He must have painted the hook and the rope black. In the near darkness, both would be invisible."

"And he must have practiced, so he could strike quickly and with deadly accuracy," said Zenta. "It was a good thing you ducked so quickly. He only missed me because I tripped on a log and fell."

The door opened and a serving girl came in with trays of food, followed by Asa. She was still very pale, and Matsuzo looked at her with concern. "Asa! You've had a shock, and you should still be in bed!"

Asa managed a smile. "I'm all right now. Everybody is happy that the dangers are over, and I want to join the celebration, too." Then her face became solemn and she bowed deeply to the two men. "Thank you for saving my life and for defending this house from attack."

Matsuzo was embarrassed. "I was almost too late to save you. Kongomaru is the real hero, and you should thank him. He saved us both."

A soft bark on the other side of the sliding door showed that Kongomaru acknowledged the compliment. Opening the door to the veranda, Matsuzo handed the dog a rice ball covered with raw fish. "Here, Kongomaru. You deserve a New Year's treat, too." Afterward, he admitted that he acted carelessly, but at the time he only felt a rush of affection for the dog.

Kongomaru devoured the tidbit in a flash and licked his jaws appreciatively. Then he sniffed and suddenly stiffened. Before anyone could move or cry out, he launched himself furiously at Zenta and knocked him flat, sending crockery and trays flying.

13

"Oh, no! Not again!" wailed Matsuzo. With Asa's help he finally succeeded in dragging the dog off. Still snarling, Kongomaru allowed himself to be pushed out of the room.

"You're a bad dog!" Asa said severely. "Why did you do that?"

On the veranda Kongomaru cringed under his mistress's scolding, but when she turned away the cock of his ears showed him unrepentant.

Matsuzo looked down anxiously at Zenta, who sat speechless, cradling his arm. It was again the right hand that suffered, and it was now bleeding from several deep and ugly gashes.

Toshi, with more presence of mind than anyone, fetched a basin of hot water, salves, and bandages. After she had bathed and bandaged the hand, Zenta regained a little color. He said to the company, "If I lose that hand, will Kongomaru leave me alone, then? Or will he start on my left hand?"

He spoke in a cold, measured voice that to Matsuzo meant that he was in a towering rage. Suffering three attacks without reason in the course of one day was too much.

Then Matsuzo remembered that there *was* a good reason for the attack. "You can't blame Kongomaru—" he began.

Zenta turned on him. "Yes, I know. Kongomaru is the hero of the hour and he saved Asa. He likes *you*." His voice rose to a snarl. "But the next time you invite him in to fondle him, please give me a chance to get out of the room first!"

"Please," said Asa, looking at Matsuzo. "Tell us why Kongomaru attacked your friend. He also jumped on you this morning. I know that he is not stupid or vicious."

"Do you remember the little scrap of cloth I picked up?" asked Matsuzo. "I was carrying the cloth when I called on you this morning, and when Kongomaru smelled it, he attacked me."

Asa nodded. Her mother said, "You told us that the piece of cloth was torn from something worn by the Cat. We know that Kongomaru hates the Cat and attacks anything connected with him. But why should he attack your friend?"

"You said that the Cat and I looked alike," said Zenta sarcastically. "Perhaps we're actually the same person?"

Asa and her mother recoiled. Since the identity of the Cat was still unknown, they had reason to be wary of

Zenta, who was after all a stranger. But he had been in the house during the siege while the Cat was attacking Asa. He couldn't have been the Cat.

"When Kongomaru attacked the Cat in the empty house just now, he tore a large piece of his sleeve," said Matsuzo. "I detected a peculiar smell that seemed familiar, and now I know why." He turned to Zenta. "It was familiar because your kimono has the same smell."

Zenta looked puzzled. His mind was probably still dulled by pain. "I bought this kimono last week, and I didn't notice anything peculiar about the smell. Could it have come from the dye?"

"I don't think so," replied Matsuzo. "I just remembered something. Kongomaru was friendly with you at first. You held out your hand to him, and he licked it. Therefore your clothes didn't acquire that smell until after he had met you in front of Ikken's house."

As the devastating implication of his own words reached him, the blood drained out of Matsuzo's face and was replaced by ice water. It took him a while to muster the courage to look at his friend, who had turned the color of raw silk. Wordlessly Zenta bowed his head and covered his eyes with his one good hand.

"Oh, Mother, the poor gentleman looks sick," cried Asa. "We'd better call the maids and have a bed laid out for him."

It was true that Zenta looked sick. He seemed on the verge of fainting. Matsuzo, who was feeling far from well himself, swallowed and said, "No, that won't be necessary. Perhaps you can leave us for a while? The victory celebration seems to be getting out of control in the courtyard. If you don't stop them soon, the villagers will do more damage than Ryutaro's men."

Toshi and Asa finally left, not without casting some worried glances behind them. When the door closed again, Matsuzo said, "It's the incense used in the tea ceremony, isn't it? It was the only thing that perfumed your clothes after we had met Kongomaru for the first time. I didn't take part in the tea ceremony, and therefore my clothes were not affected."

Zenta nodded. When he spoke, his voice sounded very tired. "I went through the tea ceremony twice, and each time we burned the same kind of incense. No wonder my relation with Kongomaru became steadily worse." After a moment he added, "You are right about the dog. He is intelligent."

Then his control broke. "Why did Ikken do it?" he cried. "He had no use for money!" He pounded his wounded hand on the floor, as if the physical pain would cover the mental anguish.

Matsuzo could not bear to look at his friend. "Perhaps he did it out of hatred. I suspect that Shunken was one of the men killed in the battle that took place here three years ago. Ikken could have been taking revenge for the death of his son."

"No, I don't believe it!" said Zenta. "The Vampire Cat murders were the work of a sadistic fiend. Ikken is the kindest man I know. I learned everything from him. He would never take revenge in this way."

"Perhaps his real nature is kindly, but a demon might have taken possession of his spirit," suggested Matsuzo.

Such cases were often described in literature and drama. There could have been an element of truth in the old tales.

"Ikken lived in fear," said Zenta. "If he was the Vampire Cat himself, why should he be so frightened every time I mentioned the subject?"

"He was afraid that the demon would possess him again," guessed Matsuzo. "He didn't know when he would commit another murder. You thought that he was afraid of the peddlers. It wasn't the peddlers he feared, it was himself."

Matsuzo began to think of other things pointing to Ikken's guilt. There was the matter of the special charcoal. Who but a tea ceremony expert would know, or care, whether charcoal was odorless? The exorcist was little better than an imbecile, and he would never have thought of using the charcoal in that way to induce faintness. Ikken must have told him what to do.

There was also the similarity in the way Zenta and the Cat moved. Zenta must have unconsciously modeled his movements on those of his teacher.

On the other hand, Matsuzo had felt that the Cat was a man in his prime. Ikken was old and frail. But Matsuzo had heard that people who were possessed had extraordinary strength and vigor. Zenta had said that Ikken had been an outstanding swordsman in his youth. While in the grip of the demon, he must have regained his skills.

No other explanation seemed possible. How else could a wise and kindly old man turn into a murderous fiend? Even Zenta couldn't seem to dispute the evidence. He picked up his swords and thrust them slowly into his sash. "This is the second time that I'm losing my father," he said quietly.

Matsuzo felt his throat tighten with pity. When he could speak again he said, "If you can't bring yourself to kill Ikken because he was your teacher, I'll do it for you."

Zenta's eyes blazed with anger. "You can't seriously suggest that I'd lift my hand against Ikken? You insult me even to suggest it!"

"But we can't allow Ikken to continue committing these murders!"

"I must see him and try to persuade him."

"Zenta, Ikken is not . . . himself. You can't find an argument that will touch him."

"You forget: there is one argument that will touch him," Zenta said.

Matsuzo fell silent. He knew that when a samurai wished to criticize his superior, he would commit hara-kiri in front of him. It was the ultimate form of reproach. "You can't do it properly with one hand," Matsuzo said huskily. "Shall I come and act as your second?"

While committing hara-kiri, it was acceptable for a samurai to ask someone to be his second—to strike off his head after he had plunged his sword into his abdomen. The purpose was to cut short the suffering. To act as a second was the duty of a friend.

"No," said Zenta. "When Ikken makes his response, I want him to be able to do it decently and privately. I don't want you there watching him like an executioner."

Matsuzo understood. The only response Ikken could make would be to commit hara-kiri in turn. Zenta wanted him to do it voluntarily, not under pressure from Matsuzo. "And what if you find Ikken in the possession of the demon? He would be blind to honor or decency, and your death might not make any impression on him."

"That's impossible!" said Zenta. "Ikken regards me as a son. I can reach him even if no one else can."

As they were leaving the house they came face to face with Toshi. She had come from tending the wounded and restoring order to her house, but she was not too busy to notice the tension in the two ronin. "There is something wrong, isn't there?" she asked. "Can I help in any way?"

"No, I'm just tired and I want to return to Ikken's house," Zenta replied calmly. "Matsuzo can stay here a little longer."

Before she could say anything more Zenta turned and walked away. Matsuzo followed him silently, and when they were outside the gate he said, "What do you want me to do?"

"Give us enough time, and then come and make sure that everything is . . . seemly. Will you do that?"

"Yes, I will," said Matsuzo steadily.

A villager ran up. "Come and look at what we found! It's Ryutaro's body!"

In his present mood Matsuzo felt like striking the man for his loud voice alone. But Zenta, even now, showed a professional interest. "Who killed him? I thought Ryutaro would be too strong for any of you."

"I don't know who killed him," answered the man. "He was already dead when we found him."

"Maybe he slipped on some ice and fell," suggested Matsuzo. "And while he was helpless the villagers attacked him."

But by the light of the flaming logs, they saw that Ryutaro had been killed by a single, powerful sword stroke. After months in Zenta's company, Matsuzo had acquired some knowledge of sword cuts. "You must have killed Ryutaro yourself without realizing it," he told Zenta. "I've never known anyone else able to make that particular stroke."

Zenta made no reply but stood looking down at Ryutaro's body with a curious stillness. Matsuzo thought at first that he had not heard. When he finally turned, Matsuzo saw that he had a strange expression on his face, a mixture of hope and a kind of suppressed rage. Even stranger were his words. "We were wrong: Ikken is not the Cat. I'm going to his house now. Come when the Hour of the Tiger strikes, and be sure to bring Kongomaru with you."

The sight of Ryutaro's wound finally told Zenta the truth. He was not the only swordsman who could make that particular stroke. There was one other: Shunken.

Shunken was the Cat. He was not dead. Ikken had lied when he said his son had been killed in battle. Somehow Shunken had survived the battle and had spent the next three years hiding in his father's house. Whether from his defeat in battle or from the strain of living as a fugitive, Shunken had gone mad. *He* was the monster, the demon who held Ikken in a grip of terror.

At the thought of Ikken's helpless terror, Zenta was filled with an intense rage. Be calm, he told himself. He had to be calm and alert, for Shunken's malevolence was now concentrated on him alone—and not just because he had frustrated Shunken's plans. This malevolence went back ten years. As an only child, Shunken had not been happy to see his father's affection given to another boy. It was Shunken's jealousy that had caused Zenta to leave Ikken's house and to delay his return for so long.

And now Zenta's return added fuel to Shunken's hatred, for Ikken must have told his son that he considered asking Zenta to marry Asa, Asa who had been betrothed to Shunken originally.

Zenta knew that he and Shunken would soon be facing each other over naked swords. That was inevitable. At fifteen, he had been unable to stand up to Shunken, who had given him lessons in swordsmanship more from a desire to humiliate than to teach. And now? Would he be a match for Shunken?

Fortunately Zenta's left hand was untouched, for that was always his stronger one. Holding his sword with that one hand, he could still make the sort of slash he had seen on Ryutaro's back. But Shunken would know about this left-handed technique, for Shunken was the one who had taught it to him.

Zenta tried to flex his right hand but found the bandage too tight to permit much movement. He loosened the bandage slightly with his teeth. It might start the bleeding again, but at least he could now use that hand if the need arose. All this time his ears were alert to catch any small sound, any hint that someone was stalking him.

The gate of Ikken's house was slightly ajar, a sign that he was expecting someone. Zenta entered without any attempt at stealth. Shunken would know that he was coming anyway. He saw that there was a light in Ikken's study. Kneeling in front of the door he said, "Sensei, I'm back. May I come in?"

"Is that Zenta? Yes, come in." Ikken's voice had a curious, breathy sound.

Gently sliding the door open, Zenta backed into the room, closed the door, and turned around. He stopped dead. The room was brightly lit by two tall candles, and Ikken was seated, crouched, rather, behind a big ceramic brazier. Above the brazier Zenta saw that Ikken was wearing pure white. The tea master was dressed for death.

"I could not afford to die before," said Ikken. "There was no one else in this village who had the power to stop Shunken and the peddler band. I still hoped that I could soothe and tame Shunken and drive the madness from his heart."

Ten years ago Ikken had succeeded in soothing and taming Zenta, but he could not do the same for his son.

The tea master had difficulty speaking. "I learned that Shunken planned to assault Asa tonight, and with the girl compromised, I would be forced to let him marry her. He had gone completely beyond my control."

"How did you learn of his plan?" asked Zenta.

"I intercepted a fugitive running for his life, the sham exorcist. I made him tell me the news, and I learned not only of the planned attack, but of the outcome. Then I knew that you had defeated Shunken." The tea master's face was serene. "You will be able to take over my responsibility. It is now safe for me to die."

"Must you die?" Zenta could not help asking the question, although he knew the answer.

Ikken nodded. "My guilt lay in not doing more to stop Shunken. Even when the evidence mounted, I closed my eyes and refused to look at the truth."

"Sensei," said Zenta, "it is not necessary for you to say any more."

Ikken went on as if he had not heard. "I knew that something was wrong when Shunken made excessive demands for money. He said he needed money to buy men and equipment, to form a new army from the ruins of the one he had lost. I had to sell all my tea utensils."

"I know, Sensei," said Zenta. "I saw your charcoal basket in the hideout of the peddlers."

Ikken nodded. "Of course. Shunken took the basket and the special charcoal. When I heard about the fainting spells of the village girls, I knew that my special charcoal had been used. Still, I refused to believe the truth."

A tremor passed over the tea master's face, but he controlled it. Looking at the charcoal brazier, Zenta caught his breath as he realized that a dark stain was spreading around its base. From waist down, Ikken's kimono was soaked with blood. The tea master was not only dressed for death, he was dying.

Suddenly Zenta couldn't control his grief any longer. "Why did Shunken do it, Sensei?"

"Because of hatred," said Ikken. "The battle here three years ago ruined all his hopes. In addition to the hideous disfigurement, his throat had been so badly injured that he could make only a thin, mewing sound. After the battle he tried to approach one of the village girls for help, but she screamed and ran away. He caught her and cut her throat."

"He told you about this girl?" asked Zenta.

Ikken nodded. "I thought that he committed the murder because he was wounded and feverish. He said nothing about the later murders."

"His rage and despair after the battle I can understand," said Zenta. "But the Vampire Cat is a cold-blooded scheme he kept up over three years! How could he sustain his rage for so long?"

The tea master's eyes had closed, but now he opened them and drew a shuddering breath. "He wanted Asa. He didn't really love her, but he was convinced that she and her money belonged to him. I refused to let her marry him."

"Was it because of the disfigurement?" asked Zenta.

"No, that wasn't the reason. A samurai's wife must learn to live with her husband's scars, however hideous. I refused to allow the marriage because after the battle I could see that the cruelty in his nature had got out of control. He had become insane."

"That was when the Vampire Cat began its campaign of terror?" said Zenta.

"Yes." Ikken's voice had become a whisper. "He needed my consent to the marriage. Asa's grandfather is giving her the money on condition that she marry a samurai of my choosing. Shunken tried to frighten me into allowing him to marry Asa. He warned that as long as she remained single, she might fall victim to the Vampire Cat. He knew that I suspected him and that the uncertainty for me was more terrifying than anything else."

Zenta remembered the fear in Ikken's eyes. It was true that Shunken's campaign was to gain certain ends, but he also enjoyed spreading terror for its own sake.

Another shudder passed through Ikken, and his face was the color of the ashes in the charcoal brazier. "Sensei, is there anything you want me to do?" asked Zenta.

Ikken looked up with a smile. "Yes. Make tea for me."

Zenta nodded and rose to fetch the utensils. To perform the tea ceremony properly, he had to achieve serenity of mind first. Forget Ikken's suffering. Forget the danger waiting outside the room. Concentrate on the beauty of the objects here: the single white camellia in the clay jar, the rough texture of the iron kettle, the ashes in the hearth, and above all the tea utensils. They were cheap, simple objects, but they had been personally selected by the tea master, and that made them priceless.

Zenta ladled hot water from the kettle and put it in the tea bowl to warm it.

He rinsed the bamboo whisk in the warm water.

He placed the ladle on top of the kettle.

He poured out the water from the tea bowl and wiped it, using a slow, gentle motion.

He wiped the tea caddy with a piece of silk cloth and at the same time wiped all impurities from his mind.

He removed the lid of the tea caddy, took three scoopfuls of the powdered tea, and put them in the tea bowl.

He felt a sharp pain as one of the gashes on his hand tore open, and his hand jerked, spilling a speck of powdered tea on the floor. Breathing slowly and steadily for a few seconds, he worked himself back into the smooth flow of the tea ceremony.

He put a ladleful of hot water into the tea bowl and replaced the ladle on the kettle, keeping the movements decisive but smooth.

He whipped the tea with the bamboo whisk, making sure that the motions were not too violent, for that would make the tea too thick.

He picked up the tea bowl with his left hand and, bowing, offered it with the right.

With bloodstained hands, Ikken raised the bowl to his lips and took a sip. The bowl fell to the floor, spilling the bright green tea into the red pool.

As Zenta bent over Ikken, the tea master whispered, "You will protect Asa from him. I know you will." Then he raised himself and spoke his last words very distinctly. "Be careful. He won't do anything as long as I'm alive, but as soon as I'm dead he will try to kill you."

Zenta caught Ikken as he fell forward and gently lowered him to the floor. Then he turned to face the door leading to the garden.

The door slowly opened and the black-clad figure of

the Cat appeared in the doorway. The voice was the thin, mewing sound he recognized, but the words were perfectly intelligible. "Yes, I'm now going to kill you," said Shunken.

14

Zenta experienced a surge of blind fury. He had never hated any man so much as he hated the man who filled the doorway. Self-control, he had to regain his self-control. Summoning all that he had learned from Ikken, he managed to quell the annihilating anger that was threatening to confuse his thinking and even blur his vision.

When Zenta spoke he was glad to find that his voice was level. "You wouldn't kill me in this room. Even *you* have enough decency to avoid that."

Zenta's words were meant to wound, and he could tell that he had succeeded. With a swift stride Shunken entered the room and jerked off the black hood that covered his head. Zenta had expected disfigurement, but still the sight of that face stopped his breath.

What had been a handsome, noble face was now cleft by a huge scar which ran from forehead to chin and then curved down across the throat. In healing, the two halves of the face did not quite come together properly, and the result was the stuff of nightmares. No one could look at that face without flinching.

Zenta must have made a sound. The hideous face suffused and the scar turned deep purple. With a high, whistling laugh Shunken said, "What do you think of my looks? You should have seen the village girls when I jumped out at them. I was able to give them quite a thrill before I killed them."

Even more than the hideous face, the high voice grated on the nerves. Looking at that ruined throat, Zenta knew why Shunken had used the grappling hook. It was to tear out the throats of his victims, just as his own had been torn.

For a moment Zenta came close to feeling pity for Shunken. Then he remembered Ikken lying in his own blood. "Your disfigurement cannot excuse your crimes," he said. "That was not the reason why your father stopped your marriage with Asa."

Shunken's respect for his father was the only human thing left in him. At Zenta's words a keening sound burst from his throat. "That's not true!" he cried. The high voice had overtones like fingernails scratching on metal. "I would have persuaded my father to let me marry Asa eventually!"

"You don't persuade, you terrorize," said Zenta. "You drove your father to his death. You killed Ryutaro. No one will feed you or shelter you from now on. You will live like a wild beast."

Because Zenta was expecting it, the grappling hook whistled harmlessly over his head as he ducked. His sword flashed out and cut clean through the rope before Shunken could retrieve the hook.

"I know all about this cheap trick," said Zenta contemptuously, as the hook clattered to the floor.

After spending his fury in physical action, however, Shunken seemed to have recovered his poise. He, too, was holding his sword in his left hand. "That was just a beginning. Do you wish to see some other tricks?"

"It would be obscene to fight in your father's tea room," said Zenta. "We must go outside."

Again Shunken gave that high, whistling laugh. "So that I'll slip and fall on the snow? I've heard about the icy patches around Asa's house. No, I have a better idea. Let's go into the practice room."

"Very well," said Zenta. He knew what the other man was trying to do. The practice room was where Zenta had taken lessons from Shunken, and in that room he would be reduced to the status of a pupil again. It would put him at a disadvantage. But this trick was one that Zenta had used himself, and he resolved not to be affected.

Sharing a lamp between them, the two deadly enemies walked side by side with their swords sheathed. They were of the same height and had the same slender build. Both walked with the springy step of the master swordsman. By an ironic coincidence, both men had been injured in the same place by the same dog, so that even their bandaged right hands looked identical. Shunken was five years older, but in the dim light the difference in ages was not noticeable, and the two men could almost have passed for each other—until one saw their faces.

In the practice room, the cold struck Zenta, numbing

him. Shunken set down the lamp and proceeded to take out some candlesticks and light them. By tacit agreement neither of the two men made a move toward hostilities. Certain things had to be said and done first.

Unlike most of the house, the practice room had been recently aired, and it shone with cleanliness. Not a trace of dust showed on the dark wooden floor, which was as smooth as a mirror. Wooden practice sticks and other weapons were neatly arranged on their racks all along the walls. Zenta suspected that Shunken spent a lot of time in the room.

Certain things were now clear to Zenta. He knew why Ikken had dismissed his servants and lived like a recluse, trying to refuse friendly overtures from Toshi and Asa. Even the rapid disappearance of food, which had puzzled Matsuzo, was explained. Another small puzzle was why the gate had been left ajar when they first arrived at Ikken's house. It had been left open for Shunken's return. It also explained why both he and Matsuzo dreamt about the Cat during their first night in the house. Shunken's mewing voice had probably reached them while they slept, causing them to have similar dreams.

Looking around the practice room, Zenta recalled the lessons he had received there from his ferociously demanding instructor. He couldn't prevent his heart from beating faster or his mouth from becoming dry, for he had suffered much pain and humiliation in this room. But he had also learned.

On Shunken's broken lips there was a frightful smile. "Will you really find the nerve to lift your hand against your teacher?"

It was a hit. To lift one's hand against one's teacher was against all sense of decency. But Zenta could hit back as well. "You are not my teacher. From you I learned only technique, nothing of the spirit. My teacher was Ikken, and I intend to avenge his death."

Shunken stiffened, and in the candlelight his eyes glowed fiercely yellow, like the eyes of a cat. "Very well. Let us begin."

Like a grotesque parody of a practice session, the two men carefully tied their sleeves back with cords and wrapped white sweat bands around their foreheads. Only this time they would not be using practice sticks.

They stooped down opposite each other, both completely motionless. "Now show me whether you remember what I taught you," said Shunken softly.

Moving so slowly and smoothly that the changes in position were barely perceptible, they rose and drew their swords. Slowly the two swords swung forward. Two paces apart, the opponents stood and faced each other. So perfect was their control that not even their breathing could be heard.

It was a silent duel, a contest of wills, as each waited for the other to make the first, revealing move. What seemed like a flicker of the eyes was only the flicker of the candles. What seemed like a trembling of the sword arm was only a fold of a sleeve blowing in the draft from a crack.

After an eternity, the break came. Zenta saw his opponent's chest rise to snatch a breath. He saw the light spill like liquid along Shunken's blade as his opponent's wrists twisted. He knew the move, and his sword whipped up and across to meet it.

It was a trick. He realized it almost too late. He was saved only by the years of cruel training he had forced himself to undergo. Doing the impossible he checked the violent swing of his sword and jerked it back down to protect his chest. The swords clashed. A gasp escaped Zenta as his right wrist was forced to take some of the impact.

Disengaged, the opponents returned almost to their original places. But now they were both breathing more heavily. Zenta could feel an icy trickle of perspiration go down his back, and he saw that two steady streams escaped from Shunken's sweat band on either side of his face.

"Not bad," remarked Shunken, as if praising a backward pupil from whom he hadn't expected too much. But Zenta knew that the speed of his recovery had shocked his opponent. There was something strained about the smile on Shunken's broken face.

Shunken had underestimated his opponent, but so had Zenta. Of late he had met no opponent of comparable caliber, and he had to stretch his abilities only when faced with overwhelming numbers. He had forgotten that during the ten years of sharpening his own skills, Shunken's would not have remained static. And Shunken had started out as his master.

Shunken's eyes dropped to Zenta's right hand. The bandage was stained and unraveling. "I see that our mutual friend has left his teeth marks on you as well," he said. "I propose that we use our left hands, only."

Zenta nodded. "It's your stronger one, anyway. You killed Ryutaro with a left-handed slash."

Again Shunken gave that harsh, scratchy laugh. "Of course. You know that stroke, because you learned it from me. I had to hurt you quite a lot before you could master it. Do you remember?"

Zenta remembered the lessons vividly. Shunken delighted in causing pain, but in the end it had driven his pupil into learning more quickly.

In spite of Shunken's proposal Zenta knew that his opponent still had the use of his right hand and could not be trusted to keep the bargain. He remembered how quickly Shunken's right hand had whipped out the grappling hook.

Not relaxing his attention from Shunken's hands, Zenta also watched his opponent's eyes. He knew, however, that someone of Shunken's caliber was capable of giving a flicker of the eyes at the wrong moment to mislead his opponent. Without seeming to, Zenta also paid particular attention to his opponent's feet. A glide or a slither sideways could tell a great deal.

Now! Shunken's weight went back on his heels, and he pivoted. This time Zenta was fully prepared for what was coming. Both men drew their second swords with their right hands and came together with a jarring clash. The sword fell from Zenta's hand with a clatter, but he had succeeded in deflecting the blow that would have cut open his chest. Tears of agony blurred his eyes, and he blinked furiously to clear them.

Shunken took the opportunity to pounce on Zenta's fallen sword and kick it out of reach. "That hurt, I think," he said. "You always did cry a lot, didn't you?"

Nevertheless Zenta saw the consternation in Shunken's eyes. It was obvious that he had not expected Zenta to survive the attack. For the first time Shunken looked less than certain of victory.

Zenta now had only one sword against his opponent's two, but he had something much more important: the knowledge that he was no longer Shunken's helpless victim. The knowledge warmed him and lent him strength.

From Shunken's throat came a high, mewing sound again, not the travesty of speech he had been using, but a keening, the sound Zenta had heard on the dark path to Ikken's house. Shunken had been driven to perfect his skills by rancor and hatred. They were no match for Zenta's, which were the result of determination and steadiness of purpose.

But hatred could still produce great power. As both men focused all their resources on the coming encounter, they knew that it would be the decisive one.

Zenta saw Shunken draw one foot in and glide the other one forward slightly. In the next instant the sword in Shunken's left hand drove down with all his strength at his opponent's face, to cleave it in two as his own had been cleft. The sword in his right hand slashed at his opponent's throat, as his own had been slashed.

And that was precisely what Zenta had been expecting. He threw himself to one side and swung his sword in a vicious arc at his opponent's waist. So great was Shunken's skill that he leaned back in time to escape the slash by a hair. But Zenta's sword looped back and flashed down in a remise no human being could have hoped to avoid.

Shunken's collarbone was broken and his right arm dangled uselessly. Although he could fight on with his left hand, he was seriously weakened by shock and pain. He was also losing blood rapidly. Still he could not bring himself to acknowledge defeat. Yielding to a former pupil was intolerable.

The opponents looked at each other, silent now except for the sound of their rough breathing. There was nothing more to be said. There was only the business to be finished.

The stillness was broken by a dog's bark at the gate. Shunken cringed. Perhaps he remembered the two occasions when he had met Kongomaru and had come off the loser. Yielding to Zenta was humiliating, but it was better than being dragged down by a dog.

It took Shunken seconds to reach the inevitable decision. Dropping to his knees, he tucked the bottom of his kimono tightly under his legs and sat back. Then he pulled open the top of his kimono and laid bare his waist. With his useless right arm it was an awkward task.

Kongomaru's barks grew louder and nearer.

Shunken looked up at Zenta and said, "Will you be my second?"

When Zenta did not immediately reply, Shunken said, "If the lessons you received from me mean nothing to you, at least do it for my father's sake."

Zenta nodded. As Shunken stabbed himself in the abdomen, Zenta's sword flashed in a great, shiny arc.

15

Asa could not be comforted. She had been deeply attached to her uncle, and she had been shocked not only by the suddenness of his death, but by the manner of it. "Why did he do it?" she cried. "He led a blameless life. He had no reason to kill himself!"

Matsuzo could hear her crying through the papered door. He and Zenta had done what they could to clean up the tea room and to arrange Ikken's body. Asa, after one look at her dead uncle, had been led out weeping to an adjoining room by her mother.

"Why did you let them come?" Zenta demanded angrily. He looked sick and gray with fatigue. "I told you to come with Kongomaru, not with the women! You must have known that you wouldn't find a very pretty scene here."

"I didn't bring them," protested Matsuzo. "I didn't even know they were coming. Toshi must have suspected something when I left their house with Kongomaru. She decided to follow me, and then Asa wanted to come also. According to Toshi, Asa was very concerned about her uncle living alone here, and at the slightest hint that something was wrong, she insisted on coming."

"We'd better not let them near the practice room," said Zenta.

Matsuzo, still stunned by the revelation of the Cat's identity, nodded soberly. "Are you going to let them know about Shunken?" he asked.

"No!" said Zenta. "Asa has had enough of a shock from her uncle's death. I can't let her discover that her beloved Shunken had turned into a murderous fiend."

Matsuzo still remembered his horror when, led by Kongomaru, he had found his way to the practice room and pushed open the door. Thinking of the ghastly severed head he said, "Since Shunken has been so badly disfigured, she might not even recognize him when she sees his face."

"We must not let her see the body at all," said Zenta firmly.

Matsuzo had a sudden idea. "Why don't we tell everyone that the Vampire Cat killed Ikken and that you came and killed him? In that way, nobody will know how Ikken really died, and there won't be any whispers or slanders about him."

"It might work," said Zenta thoughtfully. "But we'll have to get the cooperation of Toshi and Asa. They've seen Ikken's body, and they know that he committed hara-kiri."

When they went to see Asa and her mother, they found the girl still weeping.

"We could see that you were making tea for my brother-in-law," Toshi told Zenta unhappily. "Can you tell us why you did that, instead of trying to stop his bleeding and perhaps save his life?"

Seeing that Zenta was in no state to answer the question, Matsuzo answered it for him. "Ikken was a samurai. If he felt it necessary to commit hara-kiri, it was not for others to interfere."

Asa had overheard the answer. "So this is your fine samurai code of honor! It forces a wise and kindly old man to commit hara-kiri!"

"I'm sorry. We'd better go," said Zenta.

Toshi followed the two men out of the room and closed the door behind her. "This morning I would have said the same thing about the samurai. But since then I've had reason to change my mind. Hirobei respects you also, and he has no great love for the warrior class. There must have been a very good reason why my brother-in-law committed hari-kiri and why you stood by doing nothing. Would you tell me what it is?"

Toshi had changed her opinion of them, but Matsuzo had also changed his opinion of her. He had learned that she had been forced into a marriage she disliked by her social-climbing father, and she couldn't have been happy to see her daughter made to do the same thing. During the siege she had behaved with courage. Perhaps they should tell her the truth.

Zenta had come to the same conclusion. "Will you come with us?" he said to Toshi. "There is something we'd better show you."

As soon as they were out on the veranda, they could

hear Kongomaru's growls. They found him crouched in front of the door of the practice room, snarling and scratching.

"I'd better get him away," said Matsuzo hurriedly. He struggled with the dog, who stubbornly refused to move.

"Take him to the kitchen and feed him," suggested Zenta.

After repeating, "Food, Kongomaru. Don't you want to eat?" Matsuzo finally succeeded in persuading the dog to follow him.

After Matsuzo left with Kongomaru, Zenta pushed open the door of the practice room. "I'd better warn you that it's not a very pleasant sight," he told Toshi as she followed him into the room.

He and Matsuzo had unfolded a mattress and arranged Shunken's body on it. Replacing the severed head, they had covered the face with a white cloth.

Toshi knelt before the body and lifted the cloth. After one look she gasped and dropped the cloth. Then she slowly lifted the cloth again, and this time she looked squarely at the ruined face. "It's Shunken, isn't it?" she said shakily.

"He had not been killed in battle, as we all believed. Instead he hid his scarred face and lived secretly with his father."

Zenta could see Toshi's surprise change to comprehension and finally to horror. "Then he was the . . . the . . . Vampire Cat?"

Zenta nodded. "His injuries from the battle must have driven him insane."

For a long time Toshi gazed somberly at Shunken's body. Finally she looked up and said, "I see. So that's why Ikken committed hara-kiri. He held himself responsible for the crimes of his son."

Again Zenta nodded. "He had no wish to live any longer."

"Do we have to tell everyone that Shunken was the Vampire Cat?" asked Toshi anxiously. "Asa worshipped him. It would be a terrible shock for her."

"Matsuzo and I considered putting forth the story that Ikken was killed by the Cat and that we came and killed the murderer," said Zenta. "Because of the disfigurement nobody would be likely to recognize Shunken."

Toshi seemed eager to accept the suggestion. They returned to Asa and found her drying her eyes. Zenta could see the effort she was making to calm herself. Her uncle was dead, but she was trying to remember his teachings.

Toshi told Asa about the version of Ikken's death that they intended to announce. Asa nodded indifferently. "I don't know why you want to spread the story, but do what you think best. Uncle Ikken is dead; nothing else matters."

Suddenly she looked up fiercely at Zenta. "Your code is brutal and inhuman. You samurai create nothing; you only destroy."

"Asa!" said her mother. "You're talking wildly. Your grief over your uncle's death is making you confused."

"No, for the first time I'm seeing things clearly," said

the girl quietly. "I will never marry a samurai. I will marry a merchant like my grandfather."

"You're wrong if you think that would please your grandfather," said Toshi. "On the contrary, it would make him very angry, and he might disinherit you."

"I don't care if it makes him angry," said Asa.

For the first time Zenta felt a respect for the girl. Normally he only admired women with physical courage, but now he saw that Asa had something more: she had moral courage. She was prepared to defy her grandfather, even if it meant losing a fortune. How could he have ever thought her spiritless? Her resemblance to Ikken was heartbreaking.

He rose. "Good-bye, Asa," he said gently and went to the door.

Toshi followed him out of the room, her face flushed. "I'm sorry about Asa. You'll have to excuse her because of her sorrow. She loved her uncle."

"I understand," said Zenta. "I admire her spirit."

Toshi seemed a little embarrassed about how to proceed. Finally she said, "As you probably know, my brother-in-law had suggested that Asa marry one of you."

Zenta opened his mouth to speak, but Toshi went on. "I admit that I did not like the idea at first. Asa had already been betrothed to Shunken. Knowing that he was a harsh, ambitious man, I felt that she would have been very unhappy. But now I see that not every samurai is like Shunken. If you wish to marry Asa, you have my approval."

Zenta found it difficult to reply, and at his hesitation

Toshi said, "I know my father had his heart set on Asa marrying a samurai of good family, and perhaps you're afraid that your background might not meet his standards. But if Ikken suggested you, my father will give his consent."

"Asa has said that she would never marry a samurai," murmured Zenta.

"She will change her mind," said Toshi. "I can persuade her."

Zenta thought that Toshi still had something to learn about her own daughter. He didn't believe that Asa would ever change her mind.

"My friend and I lead a footloose life, and we get into adventures that could prove embarrassing to our families," he said. "I'm sure that you wouldn't want Asa married to someone disreputable."

Toshi frowned. "Of course if you have no wish to be connected with us—"

"It's not that—" said Zenta hurriedly.

"I only made the suggestion about Asa because it was Ikken's wish," said Toshi stiffly. "Now that he is dead, there is no reason why you have to respect his wish."

It was a calculated insult. Mercifully Zenta's capacity for feeling hurt had reached its limit, and he was more surprised than hurt by Toshi's words.

After a moment Toshi's eyes dropped and her face turned crimson. "Forgive me. We must seem like a very ungrateful family. After what you have done we only insult you. Please, would you honor us by staying at our house, at least until the funeral is over?"

* * *

It was the second day of New Year's, the Day for Opening the Pen. Matsuzo struggled with his New Year's poem, but inspiration would not come. He tried a phrase about snow on the winter camellias. It sounded trite. He glanced over at Zenta, who sat in a corner nursing his grief. It was not good to let him go on like that. When the door was opened by a maidservant, Matsuzo jumped up, eager for any distraction.

The girl brought news that the village was preparing a special New Year's celebration, more elaborate than anything they had had in years. In addition to drums and dancing, there would be a huge bonfire and lavish refreshments.

Matsuzo was surprised. "Lavish refreshments? I thought the people here were too poor to have anything like that."

"The villagers went to an abandoned temple which the peddlers had been using for their headquarters," said the girl. "They found a large store of money there, as well as lots of food and drink."

Zenta looked up at last and smiled. "I'm glad to hear that. Some of the people in this village have been without proper food for nearly three years. They deserve a feast."

"The villagers are wildly excited," said the maidservant, looking flushed with excitement herself. "The tavern keeper is having a party at his place, and he came in person to ask if you gentlemen could honor him with your presence."

"Shall we go?" Matsuzo asked, unable to keep the eagerness from his voice.

Zenta stood up. "All right. I don't want to miss the

spectacle of the tavern keeper being lavish with his hospitality."

Walking down the village street, Matsuzo was given a rousing reception by men he recognized as members of his ragtag army. They looked like troops greeting a general who had led them to victory. Actually, that was not far from the truth, he thought, smiling. This army of peasants and village craftsmen had overthrown a formidable band of outlaws.

The sound of drums came closer, and Matsuzo saw the lion dance weave its way down the street. A head suddenly poked out of the draperies and Matsuzo recognized the boy who had danced the lion's rear the night before.

"Come and join us!" the boy called to Matsuzo.

"Never again!" cried Matsuzo. The crowd laughed.

Turning away from the lion dance, Matsuzo thought he saw a familiar tail swish near a refreshment stall. He was not mistaken. While the attention of the stall's owner was on the lion dance, Kongomaru was taking the opportunity to snatch a morsel from a tray.

"Kongomaru!" Matsuzo called fondly.

With an I-wasn't-doing-anything expression Kongomaru jumped down from the stall and trotted toward the two ronin.

Zenta backed away nervously. "Keep him away from me."

"He won't attack you now," protested Matsuzo. "You've taken a bath and changed your clothes. The smell of the incense should be gone."

"My *mind* tells me that Kongomaru is a nice dog and

an intelligent dog and a brave dog," muttered Zenta, "but my wrist throbs when he approaches."

Matsuzo knelt and gave Kongomaru a hug. "You won't attack Zenta, will you? You're a nice doggie, you are."

Zenta looked revolted. "You'll have dog's hair all over your collar."

"Ah, you've found Kongomaru," said a voice.

Matsuzo turned and saw that it was Hirobei. The merchant looked slightly pale but was otherwise his shrewd and cynical self.

"How are your ribs?" asked Zenta.

"Sore, but improving," replied Hirobei cheerfully. "I got tired of recuperating at home, and I decided to see the fun. Since Kongomaru needed the exercise and Asa didn't want to go out, I took him with me. He disappeared as soon as he smelled food, of course."

When the three men reached the tavern, they found the owner pale with anxiety. The tavern was packed with men eating, drinking, and laughing. Nearly every time a drink went down a gullet or food entered a mouth, the tavern keeper winced. He counted the number of empty wine bottles and appeared to be doing rapid sums in his head.

The tavern keeper's wife saw the new arrivals and quickly conducted them to a separate room. "We'll give you something better than what they're getting out there," she whispered.

After she had the guests seated on cushions, she went to a little chest and took something out. It was a tiny ivory figurine. She placed it on the low table in front of Zenta and gave an embarrassed cough. "My husband finally remembered you. He recognized you as the boy who came here ten years ago and gave him this figurine in exchange for a drink. He has been feeling bad about it ever since."

"I don't believe it," said Zenta.

"Well," said the woman, "let's say his conscience bothered him now and then."

"And now he wants to return this to me?" asked Zenta incredulously.

The woman grinned. "He talked about it. That's why he took it out of storage. But every time he seemed ready to return it to you, he would change his mind. So I decided I'd better give it to you before he puts it away again."

Matsuzo's jaw nearly dropped with surprise. Zenta looked affected. He took the figurine and rubbed it gently with his fingers and then tucked it away in his sash. "Thank you," he said to the woman.

After she left the room Matsuzo recovered from his surprise. "That was probably to make up for all the bodies she looted."

The tavern keeper appeared briefly to greet his guests of honor before hurrying out again. When his wife came back with a tray of drinks, Zenta said, "Your husband doesn't seem to enjoy giving a party, does he? Why did he invite all these people, then?"

The woman's sly little eyes twinkled. "All that spear waving must have gone to his head. And when they found the big cache of money and shared it out, my husband nearly went delirious. Before he knew it, he had invited everyone in the village for a feast!"

"And now that he has calmed down, he is having second thoughts," said Matsuzo, grinning.

"Oh, well, all the money that has been shared out will find its way here eventually," said the woman. "Some people just seem to attract money."

After the tavern keeper's wife left to fetch the food, Hirobei turned to Zenta. "Have you heard that Asa now refuses to marry a samurai? Her grandfather is furious with her. He might give the business and most of his money to me when I marry Toshi."

Matsuzo could barely contain his indignation. The cunning devil! Without lifting a finger Hirobei had succeeded in getting possession of the fortune, when all of Shunken's murders and plots had accomplished nothing. Matsuzo stared at Hirobei, expecting to see some evidence of satisfaction or triumph. To his surprise the merchant looked faintly embarrassed. Or perhaps he was a superb actor.

"I think that he is leaving his business in very capable hands," Zenta said. He seemed to have something on his mind. After a moment he said to Hirobei, "I expect you to arrange a good marriage for Asa."

"Of course I will," said Hirobei.

"A really good marriage, to someone who will be kind to her," insisted Zenta. "You should provide a substantial dowry as well. It's the least you can do to make up for her loss."

"I've already made up my mind to do that," Hirobei said earnestly.

Zenta did not look entirely satisfied. "I intend to return here for a visit, to make sure that you've carried out your promise."

"You don't have to threaten me," said Hirobei. "Toshi loves her daughter deeply, and she will make my life unbearable if I don't provide well for Asa."

Suddenly the three men heard screams in the outer room. The two ronin jumped up and automatically reached for their swords. Then they realized that the screams were mixed with laughter.

The door opened and the tavern keeper's wife appeared. "They are throwing beans to chase out the devils."

Rising, the three men saw that the people were indeed throwing beans at a black-clad devil, who was running away with his arms over his face.

"Look!" cried Matsuzo. "The costume of the devil is different from the usual ones. This one is dressed like a cat!"

"So he is," said Zenta slowly. "What amazing powers of recovery these people have. Yesterday they were in dread of the Vampire Cat, and today they are already making fun of him."

"The peasants are a hardy lot," said Hirobei softly.

"Merchants are pretty tough, too," said Zenta.

"Are the samurai less hardy, then?" asked Matsuzo indignantly.

"There is something insubstantial about the samurai," murmured Zenta. "We live on what other people produce, and we only know how to destroy."

Matsuzo knew that Zenta was still thinking of Asa's words. "There must be people to destroy the destroyers," he said finally.

The two samurai put away their swords and sat down to their food.